BEAST

J. A. WYNTERS

To all the broken, the fragile, the beasts and freaks and the pretty little monsters.
You're all beautiful!

Adrian 10

I slammed the door to my new room and looked around at the bare walls.

The knock came seconds after, Dad. He was worried. These days he was always worried. He'd shrunk too. Or maybe I'd grown, or maybe it was everything that had happened in the last two years. I don't know. I didn't want to care, 'cause caring made my stomach coil and those stupid tears well in my eyes, and they made those pathetic wails crawl up my throat and close it, and that made the circles under his eyes grow a shade darker and his eyes shine. And when he thought I was sleeping, he cried too, and his face was so full of pain. His body shook really hard, and I wished there was something I could do for him, but there was nothing to do. She wasn't coming back, and we were both broken and pretending to be okay. Pretending for one another, and failing. Miserably.

"Hey buddy, you okay?" He was putting that fake happy voice on, but I felt all the fear and anxiety underneath it as slithered through the wooden door between us.

"Yeah, Dad, I'm fine," I lied.

I inhaled and he exhaled. Always going in opposite directions. We stood in frozen silence. I knew he wanted to open the door and reach in. I wasn't sure what would happen if he did.

Breaking the stillness, he said, "I'll be downstairs unpacking. Come down when you're hungry. We can have sandwiches."

"Okay." I shrugged and waited.

He stayed. I could feel him on the other side of the door. I knew what he wanted. I wanted it, too, but I was too weak to bridge the abyss of silence between us. He was the adult, he should've leapt. After a few seconds, I heard the wooden floor creak and his footsteps echo as he descended. Opportunity lost.

I should have unpacked. It would have kept my mind occupied and all those thoughts away. Instead, I sat on a box labelled *books* and stared at the empty walls. The place felt like my insides, and I didn't know how to fill it –how to start unpacking everything inside me, how to put it on neat shelves and in closed drawers and let it collect dust.

I glared at the emptiness.

A thin line of yellow light sliced the wall. My head swivelled and I glowered at my window. It was facing the house next door, and someone had just put the light on. *When had it got so dark?*

I stood up and stepped towards the window, a moth drawn to the light. I needed it all of a sudden. I pushed the window, but it didn't budge. Years of rain and weather had expanded the wood against the frame and lodged it in place.

I looked over at the house next door. It was bigger than ours and newer. A narrow slip of garden stood between the two properties, no more than six adult steps from my wall to hers. A rickety wooden fence divided the thin patch of grass which was littered with rocks and unused garden tools.

In the window stood a monster. A monster wearing a pink singlet with a red pixelated heart and jean shorts.

The monster waved.

I waved back, frowning at the strange creature.

It ripped the mask from its face. Underneath was a girl, with hair so black, light seemed to disappear inside of it. She opened her window and waved again.

I pressed against the latch. Still stuck in place. I pushed harder. Nothing. I sucked in a galvanising breath and shoved with all the force I could muster.

So many things happened all at once, all culminating in the day that changed everything.

Again.

The wood splintered around me, and the window exploded, glass shattering and twinkling like snow. I tilted forward and my world disappeared from underneath me. I floated for a split second, suspended between reality and disbelief, life and death, and in that moment, I saw an angel with eyes so blue, so icy, so beautiful they froze me in place. They held me in mid-air for longer than was possible as I fought gravity to remain locked in her stare.

Her eyes widened, coated in fear as I slipped out of my trance and gravity yanked me down to earth.

The hard ground smashed against my body, the air bursting out of my lungs in a violent retreat and my bones rattled inside me. Like a tectonic shift, everything moved and rubbed against itself. I didn't feel pain. That came later.

The world shifted, turning dark and heavy. I thought I could see the house. It was upside down, or maybe I was. A door burst open and Dad's legs drew nearer as he screamed something that could have been my name. His bare feet tainted with red as he ran into shattered glass, the hail of shards slicing his feet.

His ragged voice faded in and out. Rough hands grabbed me. I was rattled and shaken, defying gravity again as he lifted me into his arms. He might have been crying. Or maybe all those warm droplets were my blood as it gushed from everywhere.

I tasted blood, a metallic tang that coated my insides.

There were more faces and voices and a pair of brilliant blue eyes.

And then there was just darkness.

L ight seared my eyes. A sharp wail screamed around me and my body shook with vibrations inside the moving tin can. The space was cramped and there was so much noise, so much screaming. My dad's face creased with despair. A puddle of blood pooled at his feet as a man in blue uniform checked out a monitor that bleeped and moaned.

"Dad?" It was a hoarse whisper.

His head jerked up and his eyes locked with mine. Within them, I saw the worry, the fear, but most of all that question - *why?*

"It was an accident," my voice broke, saturated in despair. The disbelief on his face more brutal than the burning pain around my body.

D arkness.
      Light.
Darkness.
Light.
Stitches. So many stitches that my skin felt like a patch of embroidery.

Pain, medication, cast.

Everything…so broken.

My insides ripped to shreds. I wasn't sure they would

ever heal.

Adults spoke in code and roundabout words, but they sank in, I knew it was bad, but it could have been worse.

They used words like *luck* and *miracle*.

Maybe they were right.

After all, I did see an angel.

⁊₊

Dad pulled into the driveway in his rusted, beat-up pickup truck. It was in need of some serious love. Kind of like him, I guess. He pulled the crutches from the front seat and held on to me as I positioned my hands into the slots. He hovered as I stepped forward and kept hovering as I approached the front door.

"Dad..." I whined.

"Okay, okay!" He held his hands up and gave me a half-foot of space.

I was out of breath, and my arms burned by the time I made it into the lounge. The house looked exactly as it did the day we moved in. I guess the delay in unpacking may have had something to do with me. We both eyed the staircase as I collapsed breathless onto the couch.

Dad disappeared into the kitchen and came back with a glass of water. He handed it over and watched me as I drank. In fact, since my fall, he hadn't taken his eyes off me at all. I was sure he slept with his eyes open.

I gulped the water.

It helped.

Dad paced, carving a steady path between the mountain of boxes and idle furniture. He wrenched a hand through his hair and looked at me.

"Why, Adrian?" His face collapsed for a split second and he schooled his features into something less broken. But just slightly less.

"It was an accident, Dad. I've already told you."

"Adrian..."

"I'm not lying." Talking hurt, and not just the delicate soft centre of my inside, it physically hurt. The glass had cut my face. I knew it was deep because they said I needed over forty stitches, and I knew it was bad because no one would let me near a mirror. Every time I moved my lips, my face would stretch and twist around the wound.

"If you needed to talk to someone..."

"Dad. I didn't!" It was as if my voice wasn't even penetrating the cloud of anguish he had wrapped himself in.

"I miss her too, but you can't just—"

"I didn't!" I screamed and shot from the couch, wobbling on one foot. I grabbed my crutches, and his hands were on me. He was only trying to help, but how the hell could he help me when he couldn't even help himself?

"Get off me!" I yelled and flinched away from his touch. I shook him off, awkwardly slipping my fingers around the handles on the crutches.

"Adrian..."

I ignored him as I dragged myself to the stairs.

"Please, Adrian." His voice cracked with too much emotion and maybe that's all it took, a single crack to breach the damn and bring the whole fucking thing down.

My tears started.

They dragged from me in deep wrenching sobs as if my soul itself was bleeding. I fell into his arms and cried.

I felt his pain as I drowned in my own. A quaking as violent as mine, an undercurrent that mimicked my flood of emotion. His chest heaved as heavy tears fell from his eyes.

He dragged me to the floor. We sagged against the stairs in a quivering, drenched pile of bones and feelings all mangled and twisted into something ugly trying so hard to be anything other than broken.

I must've fallen asleep because when I opened my eyes, I was in my bed. My room was still bland and empty, but he'd made my bed with my Star Wars sheets, and I wished he hadn't. I hated them now. I only liked them because *she* bought them for me. I ground my teeth, wondering if I never called her Mum, would it hurt less.

A square of white light painted itself on the wall. It was coming in from the window.

The window.

It was intact.

Solid glass.

The original frame was gone. In its place was a thick glass window without a handle. I sat up, bracing myself on the mattress, my eyes narrowed to get a better look.

"It won't open." My dad's voice made me jerk, and my entire face spasmed in pain.

I groaned.

"Sorry."

I wondered what he was sorry about. I had a list a mile long of owed apologies.

I let it go.

For now.

He approached my bed and handed me a glass of water. "Here." He offered me two pills from his other hand. "For the pain."

I took the pills and felt them scratch my throat as they rolled down into the vast emptiness inside me. Maybe they could numb that too.

"We need to put some cream on your face. The doctor said to keep it moist..."

"I want to see..."

"I'm not sure that's a goo—"

"I want to see, Dad."

His face twisted, creasing his brow. "Adrian."

"You can't keep me away from a mirror forever."

He exhaled heavily and nodded, swiping a hand over the growth on his chin. "You're right. How about we get this cream on and have some breakfast, and maybe after that you can unpack your room a little..."

"Dad."

"Adrian Rose! Just do what you're told." He pushed me down onto my pillow and the tube of ointment appeared in his hand like magic. "Lie down!"

I pushed my head back, sinking against the pillow. Clenching my jaw hurt, and so did pouting or frowning. I slammed my eyes shut as he covered my face in the thick, white cream. It smelled like old men and wet nappies. It wanted to gag.

"Breakfast, then your room, then we can talk about it."

I grumbled my answer and he released me, the corners of his eyes creasing.

As soon as he was out of my room, I grabbed my crutches.

First, I was going to look.

I twisted the handle of the bathroom and gazed at the wall where the mirror should have been. My heart smashed against my chest with the same ferocity that my body had hit the ground. A rectangular cavity greeted me. The paint flaked off the wall like diseased skin where the glue had been peeled away.

I stared at the broken patch and tightened my grip on my crutches. My knuckles turned white.

⁓⊷⊕

My body wanted to heal, but the sweat and pus that leaked from it at night glued the sheets to my skin, eliciting agonising tearing sensations with every movement.

Dad would be at my door each morning and help me into

the shower, where the scalding water helped peel away the sheets, my skin, my blood, my tears.

My body screamed and cried, tearing away at itself every day. Long, angry streaks covered every part of me. I knew when they healed, they would leave long, angry marks everywhere, wrapped like ivy around me. My body knitted itself into knots, as I wondered what my face might look like.

I screamed in pain, and my dad just washed and scrubbed, washing away his problems. Me.

Ten days.

Ten days of excruciating pain and long silences. I think they were worse than all the rest of it. My fall created a divide between us that he had no idea how to cross.

We both stared at our half-eaten breakfast.

"Are you ready?"

I nodded. "Yes."

"Let's go."

My skin crawled with tension as we drove. He turned the radio dial, trying to fill the empty space between us.

The doctor's office was typical, full to capacity with the sick and elderly, screaming children and tired mothers. Everyone crammed into a small, hot room that cultivated more sickness and anxiety.

Dad's foot tapped on the white tile, and his hands laced together, twisted and mangled. I felt eyes—they followed me everywhere. Each time I looked up, I caught them snatching a glimpse, looking in horror, fascinated by the grotesque. The seat next to mine remained vacant, people avoided me as if I carried the plague, their eyes boring into me, then flinching away as if afraid.

A small kid pointed, and all I wanted was to grab my dad's hand and for him to tell me it was all going to be okay. He didn't. His eyes drifted into a glazed trance, as if he wasn't even there.

The doctor pulled the stitches out one at a time, I could

feel the thread as it slithered under my skin. My shoulder, my back, the rounded slice around my hip, and then my face. Agonisingly slow. I clutched the edge of the bed and stared at a mouldy black spot on the ceiling.

"All done. Adrian, you were very brave."

"Can I see now, please?"

His eyes shot to my dad, who froze.

"Can I see you outside?" The doctor smiled at my father, who was already stepping over the threshold.

I heard their voices as they filtered under the door. *Already been through so much... he won't handle it... he will see it eventually... better sooner than later.*

My good leg swung off the edge of the bed as I ran a hand over my face. It felt raw and strange. I traced the long dip that ran from my scalp across my cheek, it clipped the edge of my lip and continued down to my chin.

My dad burst into the room. "Let's go." He reached for my crutches.

"No! Not till I see."

"Adrian."

"No!" I wasn't waiting another six weeks.

"Doctor Cline has other patients."

"I don't care. I need to see. Please," I begged, and felt the tear as it burned a trail down my cheek.

My dad scrubbed a hand over his face and sighed, his shoulders slumping, "Okay." He tipped his head in surrender, and there it was in his eyes, dread. It drenched him like a thunderous downpour.

We stood outside the toilets. I smelled the disinfectant and other people's piss. It was gross, and probably not the ideal place to see my new face for the first time, but desperate times call for desperate measures. I didn't want to take the chance that Dad might change his mind at any second, having gone to ridiculous lengths to shelter me from my own reflection.

"Are you sure?" His voice was grave and full of trepidation.

I nodded, my heart climbing its way up my throat.

"Are you ready?"

I ground my teeth and drew a breath. *Now or later or never?*

Now.

Dad pushed the door, and I stepped inside. I gasped, half in horror, half in surprise as I saw myself in the giant mirror, frozen in place. For a split second, I took it all in, not really absorbing what I was seeing. I couldn't move, or maybe I didn't want to. I knew once I had a closer look, it would all be real. Maybe the shock was there to protect me from what awaited. But then Dad started talking, and the shock fell away, shattering around me like glass.

"The doctor said it will become lighter in time," he stammered. "They all will." Dad gestured to my body, but all I could see was my face—or what used to be my face.

It was now carved by a long, angry ravine that stretched from my scalp to the tip of my chin.

I took a few steps closer and examined my new souvenir. I gripped the edge of the sink, my knuckles blanching, and stared at my reflection. The long, jagged scar that snaked along my face wasn't smooth, but rough and crude.

I unclenched one hand and feathered my fingertips over the disfiguring wound, trying to find my own face in the two carved halves. Where Doctor Cline had pulled out the stitches, tiny dots decorated both banks of the scar tissue like deformed Christmas lights.

I turned away, no longer able to look at the creature standing where I should be. I bit my quivering lips, holding my pain inside. Willing my tears to dry up.

I saw Dad in my periphery, jerking his hand into the air, as though he might want to pat my shoulder or pull me in for a hug. Instead, it hovered like a fly between us, then he plunged it into his hair. His mouth stretched into a grim line buried in his stubble.

"Are you ready?" His voice cracked a little, and he cleared his throat, moving back towards the door.

I nodded, because if I opened my mouth, I would have screamed. My limbs moved as if someone else was controlling them. I was a marionette in some pathetic, tragedy.

The drive home was a blur. I knew he was saying words, but I couldn't hear him. I didn't want to. My chin hung on my chest as I looked at my feet. I knew he wanted to comfort me, but all I could see was blame. He thought it was my fault. That I did it to myself. I deserved this. He'd never say it out loud, but I'd seen it in his eyes every day since we came home. I deserved it for doing this to him.

I clenched my fists and grabbed the seat, feeling something inside me snap. I could almost hear it, like a dried-out branch.

I cracked. And I'd never be the same again.

⚓

"Get dressed and come down for dinner."

"I'm not coming," I yelled back at him.

It was almost the end of the summer vacation, and I'd spent almost all of it inside these four walls. Before we moved, Dad had had grand plans for us. The beach and local pool. There was a mountain he wanted to hike. I think he wanted to fill our days with activities rather than silence and grief… So much for that.

It took him two seconds to knock on my door.

"We're having guests over."

"Well, in that case, there's no way I'm coming down."

He sighed. He'd been doing that a lot lately. That and drinking and crying—sometimes all three at once, mostly when he thought I couldn't see, or hear, or smell him.

He stepped into my room. His nose crinkled, and his eyes shot to the window.

"If I could open it, it would smell better," I said.

He ignored me and came to sit on the edge of my bed. My eyes were still locked on the wavering spider web that was hanging loosely from the ceiling. I'd been waiting for days for it to detach itself and fall.

"Please don't make this more difficult. It's just the next-door neighbours. They helped when you…" He grimaced, stumbled over his words, and tried again. "When you had your fall."

"I don't want to see anyone."

"Adrian, please."

He raked a hand through his hair, and I finally looked at him. He looked worn down, tired. I was a bit taken aback by how much he had aged in the last few months. I wanted to be selfish and stubborn, but I hated seeing him like this. He used to have laughter lines—now they were all creased from stress and worry and pain.

"I'm leaving as soon as I'm done with my food."

"Fine."

He seemed relieved. I didn't feel like such a terrible son, anymore. I wondered if he felt less like a shit dad.

A while later voices drifted upwards, and I steeled myself.

"Adrian, our guests are here."

I hobbled downstairs, my mouth set in a scowl, my jaw clenched. If they wanted to come over for a freak show, I would give them one.

My dad stood at the door, with two other adults. The brown-eyed woman held a casserole of some sort that I was determined to hate, but it smelled amazing. My heart pinched at the betrayal even as my stomach growled. I wasn't going to touch it. The man was broad and neat, like a Ken doll that had just been unboxed.

I was about to do a U-turn and call the whole thing off

when my dad saw me and his face split into a smile that
threatened to crack me open.

"There you are. Come here and meet Mr and Mrs
Savage." His gaze swivelled to the woman at the door, I didn't
care what her name was. "And this is their daughter…"

"Tove," the woman said.

Before I could do anything stupid, a girl squeezed her
way from between the adults and walked towards me.

The girl from the window. My monster, my angel.

I growled at her and clawed on the railing, pulling myself
upstairs. I ignored my father's calls. He sounded helpless,
upset. I guess we'd be having a talk about this later. I didn't
care.

Tove.

The name of my enemy.

A beautiful, raven-haired, blue-eyed enemy who smiled at
me. What was wrong with her?

I slammed my door shut, and the voices drifted up to my
room, as did the smell of that casserole. My stomach
rumbled, and I ignored it. I'd go down later when Dad slept
and grab something from the fridge.

My door swung open, and there she was, at my door, not
asking for permission. She just crossed the threshold and
closed the door behind her. "Your dad told me to just come
on up, so here I am."

I ignored her.

She walked around my room, looking over the bookshelf
and posters, my old athletics trophies and bed.

"You have a nice room."

"Don't touch my stuff."

"Well, I can't really not touch your stuff if we're stuck in
here together."

"You're not stuck. You can leave anytime you want."

"So can you." She shrugged as if it was that easy. I
suddenly became aware that she hadn't flinched away from

me or said anything at all about my face or arms or legs. Did all my scars turn invisible?

I touched the ravine ripping my face in two. Nope. Still there.

"What's your problem, anyway?"

I swivelled to look at her. Her hands were folded across her chest, and her mouth drifted to the left in a pout.

"Why didn't you tell them?"

"Tell them what?" Her brow creased.

"That I fell."

Her icy eyes grew wider for a split second, then her hands dropped to the sides. "I did, they just didn't believe me." She shrugged and fell onto my bed, bouncing lightly as she did.

It was as simple as that. They didn't believe her, in the same way they didn't believe me. Except that she had accepted it as what adults do, while I sat and unwound the knot of anger and confusion that had knitted itself into my brain.

Just like that, Tove made a place for herself in my room, in my house, and maybe, just maybe in my heart.

⁓✈

The rest of summer suddenly flew by. Tove was over almost every day, dragging me out of my room and into the godforsaken sun. People looked. They looked at me, they looked at her, they looked at her being with me, and it felt okay, safe. She was like a shield. When she was around, I didn't feel the stabbing looks or the whispers crawl inside my ears. And never, not once, did she mention my fall or my face.

It was the best summer ever.

Tove 13

Mum slipped her hand into mine and looked at me in that way she did. The way where she could still see me. I squeezed her hand and felt the warmth of it.

"I have something to tell you." She gave me a wan smile and my heart looped around my chest."What is it?"

"Your dad and I decided that it's best if I move."

"Move? Where? Why? Are you guys breaking up?"

"No darling, no." She tucked an errant strand of hair behind my ear and her face did that thing where she was trying to pretend everything was okay when really, nothing was okay.

I braced myself.

"I'm going to move to Abbertsfield. There's a facility there…"

"No! You can't!"

"Tove."

"No! Stay here, I can take care of you, I promise."

She smiled and skimmed my chin with her smooth warm

hands, wiping away my tears, smearing them across my skin like war paint.

"You'll be okay."

"I won't! I need you."

She bit her lower lip and cleared her throat. "I'm not me anymore, sweetheart. If I stay, I will end up hurting you."

"No, Mum, you won't."

"Sweetheart, I know it's hard, but this will be best for all of us."

"No, it won't!" I flinched away from her and screamed in her face, "It's just good for you, so Dad can be at work all the time and you guys can just live your own lives without me."

"You know that's not true." She remained calm, but I saw her face crumple a little more. "Your dad will take care of you."

"The way he takes care of you?"

Her hand cracked across my face, snapping it back with the force of her blow. I jerked my hand up to the searing skin where heat saturated my cheek.

Her hand shot to her mouth and her face creased with remorse. "Oh sweetheart, I'm sorry."

I stood there, shaking. My hand glued to my burning cheek, my eyes welling with angry tears.

"What good is all his money if none of it can make you better anyway?" I hissed through clenched teeth and ran upstairs, slamming the door in my wake.

I sat at my desk swiping away unshed tears. I wasn't going to cry for her. A flicker of movement caught my eye and I saw Adrian pacing in his room. His shirtless skinny body was covered in marks. His face pensive and sullen.

I grabbed my marker and a clean sheet of paper and started writing. I loved communicating with Adrian this way. I loved the silence that came with our words. As if they belonged only to us.

It started after the summer holiday ended three years ago.

The first day of school was hard on him. There were stolen uncomfortable looks and a few whispers, after I put everyone in their place, they accepted that Adrian wore scars across his face and body, and beneath them, he was just as confused and angry as the rest of us. Nothing more.

That afternoon, I found him just staring into my window. It wasn't freaky or terrifying. He just looked so sad. I looked at him and asked if he was okay, he pulled a face, and then shook his head. I tried again and he shrugged, pointing to his ear. I sighed and scoured my room until I found a sheet of paper and wrote, '**what?**'

He shook his head at me.

I slapped that piece of paper on my window again and pointed at it. He disappeared. The paper fell from my hand like a leaf and I was left to stand staring into the empty square. I felt a surge of disappointment, like ants crawling all over my skin, but then his shadow darkened the window and his shape appeared, holding a marker and some paper.

It was my favourite time of day, watching his brow furrow as he scribbled something totally unintelligible for me to interpret. But it was never his words he was sending me, there were so many other things on that page. All his pain and wrath and trust and fear. And all I wanted was to shatter that window and reach inside and hold him, hear his heart beat all around me and tell him that it would all be okay.

'**I'm not in the mood.**' He slapped the message on his window, his terrible handwriting worse than usual. He watched me as I deciphered his scribbles then waited for my answer.

'**So what else is new?**' I took my time writing with my new hot pink marker, each rounded letter perfectly legible. I knew it bothered him. Not my writing, but the time it took me to compose anything. Not in a bad way, just that it kept him waiting, and he'd grown very impatient. He was always in a hurry, a hurry to leave, to disappear, to go where other people are not. I got it, I did, but I had been having a hard time keeping up with him. Adrian's mouth flickered in a smile. His smile made his face move, but it wasn't his fault. The scar tugged his skin in every direction, it made his whole face change and twist. It was freaky and beautiful all at once.

I'd never thought of Adrian as ugly. In fact, he was the most beautiful guy I knew, and he made me laugh, and he made me forget my parents. Or rather, he made me forget that they kept forgetting about me.

He bent over again and wrote. 'Dad says I can have a phone for my birthday.'

'Mine too,' I wrote back. His face lit up and he smiled at me through the glass. We'd been counting down the days till we were both fourteen. Once we got phones it would be easier to read his writing and our notes wouldn't be lying around to be discovered...not that our parents really cared. **'Want to go to the lake tomorrow?'**

'Sure.' He held the paper against his window.

I smiled. It was thin and pathetic and about to break as I waved goodbye.

He waved back and I threw myself onto my bed, soaking my pillow.

Adrian

I woke up too early, feeling the discomfort in my shorts. My ears burned. My body was losing control of itself. I lay in bed seeped in darkness, and tried to think about anything other than spending the day with Tove. My mind refused to budge.

I didn't want to admit it to myself but spending time alone with Tove was quickly becoming my preferred pastime. Much more than usual. I'd always kind of loved her, in her annoying sort of way. Ever since the day she invaded my room. She was like a pop up on a computer screen that kept asking if you wanted to buy the upgraded version. No matter how many times you declined, the bloody thing would pop up again. So, she stuck around, and I liked it, far more than I should have.

But it was only in the last year that I started liking it in a very different way. Tove didn't just make me happy, she didn't just make me laugh. She made my entire body feel different, because her body became something different too. Whenever she touched me, my skin heated and everywhere felt tighter and harder. I became aware of things about her that a year ago went unnoticed. Like the way her mouth tipped to the right when she smirked and it made my stomach twist, and the way she flicked her hair made my body ache and the way she ran her fingers along my arm made me want to lose control and do strange things.

It was getting too hard to control, but being with Tove meant being happy. An escape from school, and Dad's moods, and homework, and a pile of other shit I didn't want to deal with. On weekends she wasn't the most popular girl at school, she was just my friend, and I got to have a hundred percent of her attention.

I changed out of my stained pants and sweaty shirt and sat in my dark room watching her window, waiting for the sun to chase away the night. For her light to flicker on and her groggy smile to greet me.

I must have fallen asleep waiting, 'cause next thing she was jumping on my bed and screaming in my face. "Wake up sleepyhead!"

Her nose grazed mine and her blue eyes curved at the edges, a happy smile plastered across her face. It only lasted a second as my stupid body betrayed me. Her eyes grew wide as she felt my hard cock against her. She jumped off me, yelping.

"I'm sorry," I stammered and felt the heat rise to my face and burn my ears. "I have no control over it."

She stood motionless, for maybe a full minute and stared at my shorts, then burst out laughing. At the sound, my erection deflated and hid behind a new growth of hair. I felt my whole body burn.

"Come on, sunlight's wasting." She turned away and walked out of my room.

She was good like that, Tove, she let me live everything down. She never mentioned my scars, or my hard-ons or any other fuck ups. She laughed it off or shrugged then moved on. She just took me as I was. It was the most incredible fucking feeling.

The sky was so blue. It was as if the world ran out of all the other colours, leaving just a monotone strip of light blue that hung above us. It was a perfect day. We walked to the lake.

Tove was unusually quiet. It wasn't like her to keep her mouth closed. She always talked about stuff that didn't really matter… well, not to me, anyway. I think that even if she never really said it, she thought I was missing something by not having as many friends as her. I think she was trying to make me part of something bigger, but when I was with her, I already felt that I was.

I nudged her. "What?"

"Nothing." She looked down at her feet as we carved through Mr Cunningham's backyard.

"Tove?"

"It's nothing."

"Tove." I stopped walking.

She took a few more steps than swivelled towards me.

"Come on, Adrian, Mr C will kill us if he finds us here."

"I'm not moving till you start talking."

"Adrian." Her voice carried a nervous undercurrent and her head swivelled back and forth.

I shrugged, then folded my arms across my body. What could Mr Cunningham do anyway? Beat me up? Scar me some more? I couldn't possibly get any uglier.

I heard the creak behind me, but my eyes remained fixed on Tove. Colour drained from her face and her eyes grew wide.

"Get the fuck off my property you little assholes," the hollow voice screamed at us.

"Adrian come on," she panicked, "we have to go."

"Are you going to talk?"

"Adrian."

I followed her gaze and saw Mr Cunningham walk out of his house wielding a shovel. He swung it around over his head and took off towards us. "Get off my property, you runts."

"Adrian!" Her body tensed, ready to bolt, "Okay, okay, I'll talk, now come on!" She took off squealing and I darted after her, Mr Cunningham swearing at us as we snuck through the gap in the fence and erupted onto the sandy lane that led to the lake.

We ran until we were out of breath. We stopped gasping for air and giggling madly, her face painted pink, adrenaline surging inside me in a rising tide.

"You're insane." She pushed me and giggled.

"'Cause I have nothing to lose."

Her face scrunched up.

"That's very dramatic."

I shrugged and started walking again. Tove fell into step next to me.

"So?"

She sighed. "Mum's leaving."

"Leaving?"

"To a *facility*, in Abbertsfield."

"When?"

"Soon…" Her lip trembled.

"Are you okay?"

"I don't know." Her voice quivered, and she stopped walking. "I wish she was dead." Her voice seeped with venom.

"Tove!"

"What? At least your mum didn't choose to leave you."

"Don't…"

Her body crashed against mine, her arms wrapped around me squeezing, her tears staining my shirt. I wrapped my arms around her, drawing her close. Her smaller body shook and quivered and despite her misery, my stomach fluttered at the feeling of her body pressed against mine. "Tove…"

She pushed away and wiped her face on her shirt, allowing me a glimpse of her abs. "Sorry. I shouldn't have said that."

"It's okay. You can't help the way you feel."

Her eyes held mine. "No, I guess not."

Something in the way she looked at me made my body harden and twist. I turned away from her and continued walking, the slight breeze cooling my heated face, carrying with it the smell of suntan lotion and exhaust fumes from jet skis tearing up the water.

The lake was crowded as it often was on a sunny Saturday morning. People scattered around the shore, noisy chatter and distant engines carried across the choppy murky water.

We swam, then ate the sliced watermelon my dad packed up for us. Tove giggled as she bit into the fruit, her teeth sinking into the red flesh, her lips sucking the icy wetness. My eyes trailed the dripping juice as it ran down her chin and dropped onto her thigh. She swiped at the drop with a finger and sucked on it, her red lips tightening around the digit, then it popped out with a soft sound that made my body want to do things again. Fighting it was becoming unbearable. It was beautiful agony watching her eat that damn thing. I wrenched my gaze away from her, unable to withstand the suffering.

"Are you okay?" she asked.

My gaze travelled the length of her and landed on her mouth. Glistening, drenched in juice. Tove's tongue darted out and licked her lips then sucked the lower one into her mouth, releasing it ever so slowly. My gaze flickered to her eyes that grew a fraction wider as if all my thoughts were written across my body, and maybe they were. I felt the wonderful, terrible swelling start to grow between my legs, and that's when she did it.

She leaned in, and my world tilted as only Tove could make it tilt.

Tove Savage. Leaned. In. To. Kiss. Me

And all my thoughts evaporated. In an instant I was nothing but a cloud made of air and swirling wind as her lips touched mine.

Just her lips, there was no time for anything else, and I'd never know if there could have been anything else because just as it had started it ended. But not beautifully and soft – it ended in an instant, like something severed by a butcher's knife.

It was the snickers that pulled her away from me. Tove's lips ripped away from mine and we looked up to find Nikki and Romy, standing just behind us. They pointed and laughed and Nikki cringed and shrieked, "You're kissing that freak? Tove, what the hell is wrong with you?"

Somewhere deep inside of me, I hoped that when she stood up it would be to tell them to go to hell. Instead, she snatched her towel, covered her bikini clad body and looked at me with disdain, as if it was the first time she noticed who I was, as if my scars disgusted her, as if *I* disgusted her. She was looking at me through their eyes.

Tove wiped her mouth with the back of her hand. "*He* kissed *me*. I felt sorry for him, I mean… look at him."

They giggled as humiliation rose through my core and flushed through me.

The girls ran off. The words *charity case* and *pathetic freak* hung in the air.

Tove's pink singlet lay next to me, crumpled and discarded like the moment we shared, like my heart. It felt tainted now, sullied. I ground my teeth and watched them disappear into the distance, blending with the rest of the crowd.

I grabbed my towel shielding my erection. Because life was hard enough. I stood up, all my muscles quivering. My pulse surged, pumping searing rage throughout my body.

I hated Tove Savage.

I hated Nikki and Romy and my dad.

I hated everyone.

I shuffled home, trying to forget Tove fucking Savage. Trying to forget how sunshine spilt from under her glowing skin, how her lips felt on mine. Soft and warm, and wet with watermelon juice that grew sticky as the sun caked it on my face.

By the time I got home the humiliation had curdled into something grotesque and twisted. Anger and fury burned my insides, my knuckles blanched as my fists tightened by my side.

I pushed past my father whose smile fell away when he saw my face, and took the stairs two at a time before slamming the door to my room.

I ignored his gentle knocks till he left, then lay on my bed. The cold sheets chilling my burning skin. I wanted to break everything, punch holes into the walls and break myself against something so that the pain would soften. Instead, I swallowed it whole, tasting it. The flavour of the watermelon had soured on my lips and glazed the inside of my throat. All

I wanted was to throw up. I gripped my sheets and sucked in breath, one after another, after another.

Dad called me for dinner, but I wasn't hungry.

I left my room for a piss, and when I got back, there she was, at the window, waving at me. As if nothing had happened.

I ignored her and lay on my bed.

I ignored her for five whole days. I'm not sure who suffered more because even though I hated her I loved her too. I missed her every second. Missed her annoying voice and stupid smile and not so girly body and ridiculous conversations. But she had to know just how much she'd hurt me. I caught her lingering looks at school, her eyes begging for forgiveness. Punishing Tove was the kind of torture I was willing to endure.

On the fifth day I waited by my window. I was going to say everything I had to say and get it out of my body. The anger was like poison, strangling me and I was suffocating on it.

Her smile was so bright when she saw me that my resolve almost melted away, but I had my papers and my words, and I was ready.

What I didn't expect was that she would have hers, too.

We slammed our papers on our windows at the same time:

'I'm angry at you.' 'I'm sorry.'

We both read the exchange and raised the next sheet.

'You're mean!' 'I shouldn't have done that.'

I had so many more papers, more insults, but instead, I read her words and flipped over my paper to scribble a new note. She watched. **'Which part?'**

She scrunched her face and I scribbled on. **'Do you regret? The kiss or after?'**

My heart slammed against my chest as I watched her write so painfully slow. My nails dug into my palm as I held my breath. I wanted to pretend that I didn't care what her answer was, as if my world wouldn't end if she said it was the kiss. As if I wouldn't fall into a sad and pathetic black hole of self-loathing and loneliness if my best friend decided that kissing me was a mistake.

Her response seemed to be taking forever, the paper in her hand floating upwards like a snowflake fighting a harsh wind. Then, the paper crashed against the windowpane and my heart seized for just a second as I read the word, searing it into my retinas.

'AFTER!'

The word scorched itself into my skin and I felt the tension and anger trickle away from me, even as I wished I could hold on to it.

Tove smiled at me and blew me a kiss. Then drew her curtains, bringing our conversation and fight to an end.

Adrian 16

I fucking hated Tray King. If ever there was a douchebag to be crowned as king, he fit the bill in every way. In fact, his name practically gave him the title. King douchebag. Tove hated it when I called him that, but I didn't give a shit, the guy was a fucking monster. A broad shouldered, six foot two, sandy haired perfect fucking monster.

Dad kept saying I had a late growth spurt, that it would come, but I think he was just trying to make me feel good about the fact that I hadn't filled out. My scrawny build was pitiful. Although I was taller than Tray, I looked like I had been stretched out on a medieval rack, my arms like rubber bands.

Tray moved into town at the beginning of the year. Everyone else grew up here. Grew up with me. They had always just accepted that I was the kid with the giant red rip through his face, but Tray, he took it upon himself to make torturing me an art form. He was the king at school and all his minions followed him like lemmings. I wished he'd lead them all off a cliff.

I raked a hand through my hair and stepped inside the house, wanting the day to be over. Dad stood by the front door waiting for me. As with every other day, his smile faltered when he saw me.

"Dad, what are you doing home?"

"Happy birthday, Adrian."

"Thanks." I gave him a quick smile and side stepped him, marching up the stairs. I didn't care much for celebrations. Not really. Since Mum, and the accident, they'd always been a quiet affair. Dad tried to throw me parties, and asked me to invite some friends, but even though no one really said anything, I sensed it on them, the desire to keep away from me as if my scars would somehow infect them. The way they never touched me when we sat near each other in class or flinched if we accidentally rubbed skin, wiping themselves. I was malignant. Only one person touched me. She wasn't afraid or disgusted. She made my skin tingle and my heart stumble every time her fingers feathered over my arm or her body leaned against mine

At the beginning, Tove used to talk Tray and his gang of monkeys down. A word from the most popular girl at school and they all let me be. But high school is like the savannah, predators around every corner waiting to tear you apart, and Tove had to survive just as much as I did. Her affiliation with me, minute as it was, was detrimental to that. So, we ignored each other, pretending the other didn't exist. She shot me apologetic looks as she'd walk by me in the hall.

Tove was theirs during the day, but at night, when darkness came, she was all mine. I was her dirty little secret, the monster she kept under the bed— the skeleton she hid in her closet. Unseen. Unknown. I hated it, but I needed it like a dirty, ugly addiction. If that was all I could have of Tove, I would settle.

I knew how she felt, who she was. With me she was real. With them she was an unrecognisable version of herself. But it was the version she chose to be in the daytime when the sun was out. A cold-hearted bitch. At night her heart would melt, and she would be all mine. Just like she used to be.

I opened the door to my room and froze, staring at the single red bow stretched across my window. My dad came up behind me.

"What's this?"

"Open it."

"You mean…?'

"It's time."

I let my backpack drop to the floor and walked over to the window on shaky legs. I yanked the bow from the new window frame and curled my hand around the new handle. It felt cool in my sweaty hand. My breathing faltered as I twisted and pulled. The window slid across, and fresh air flowed into the room, carried by an afternoon breeze airing my room for the first time in seven years.

I sucked in a deep breath, but the air refused to get into my lungs, as though they were being squeezed by tight rubber bands. I closed my eyes and let the breeze play on my face, my hands gripping window frame as my brain tried to comprehend these feelings. It felt like happiness, but more. It inflated, expanded, overwhelming. Like I'd lit a match and someone threw petrol all over it.

I turned to my dad, my body saturated with warmth. It flooded through me. For a second my eyes found his face, the lines carving out his uncertainty. I smashed against him and wrapped my arms around his strong body. We stumbled backwards a few steps, and I heard the air falling from his mouth, but he folded his arms around me, and held tight, as if I was a ledge and he was about to fall, drawing me into him.

It was the first time I'd hugged my dad since I fell. Seven fucking years. Maybe him giving me a window could also open a door for us. Maybe he finally trusted me again, though I didn't think he'd ever believe me.

His eyes glistened with tears when he pulled away and I gave him an embarrassed smile, my heart crumbling a little at the sight of him.

"Maybe we can go out for dinner later?" His voice was unsteady.

"I'd rather stay in."

He nodded. "Take-away and *Die Hard*?"

"Sounds good, Dad."

His lips curled into a smile, and his whole face lit up. I could almost see the excitement as it bloomed inside of him, like I was the one that had given him a gift.

When he left, I went to sit by my window, just breathing, seeing the world in full, multi-coloured tones, not through a pane. It looked much the same, but it was completely different. I could smell the outside world and feel the light breeze as it cooled my room and tickled my skin. I wished I could tell Tove.

Fucking Tove. She was probably with King Douche. The thought sent shivers down my spine and the happiness began to leak from me and out the open window.

It was the natural course of events that the most popular girl in school would date the most popular guy. But every time I saw her with him my body tensed and coiled. I hated the thought of his hands all over her.

They should have been my hands.

Tove was like the wind that drifted into my room. She was everywhere inside of me. I felt her and yet no matter how hard I tried I couldn't hold on to her. Not in the way I wanted, not in the way she deserved. My hands clutched the window frame and I looked down. Falling would be so easy.

The thought evaporated as Dad called me for dinner. I pushed away from the window, slamming it shut.

The curry burned my tongue and rivulets of sweat dripped from my forehead, running down to my chin.

My phone rang somewhere between *'Ho Ho Ho'* and *'now I have a machine gun.'* Tove. I ignored it.

Dad gave me a sideways glance.

"You're not going to pick that up?"

"Nope."

"She might want to wish you a happy birthday."

I shrugged. "She might." I cocked my head and locked eyes with Hans Gruber on the screen.

Dad shifted his weight and I could feel his eyes on me. The weight of all our unspoken words sat on the couch beside us, cramping the space, pushing against us like unwelcome visitors.

Dad shoved a hand through his hair and just as predictable as always, turned back to the screen and flopped back onto the couch like a puppet whose strings have been chopped off.

When the phone rang a second time he didn't even look up. It vibrated between us like all our inconvenient truths and heavy silences.

When the movie ended, I threw the empty take-away containers in the sink and made to go upstairs.

"Adrian?" Dad called out, his face torn.

"Yeah?"

"Happy birthday, son."

"Thanks." I turned to walk away.

"I'm sorry."

"Don't worry about it." I climbed the first step.

"Adrian…?"

"Yeah?" I turned to look at him again and his face swas shredded in uncertainty. I could feel all the emotion as it coursed between us, years of silence.

He gripped the back of his neck as he stood looking

uncomfortable. An awkward, wan smile hung in the middle of his tortured face. "I'm proud of you."

"Thanks." I shrugged and left him there at the bottom of the stairs to ferment in his own guilt. Maybe the window was his apology, his truce, the bridge across our great divide, but it felt too little, too late. We were both just sad tragic men who couldn't admit how much we'd fucked up and how much we needed each other to recover. I guess today wasn't going to be any different.

As soon as I switched my light on my phone vibrated.

The screen glowed with her pathetic apology. **'I'm sorry about today.'**

Why was everyone apologising to me today?

The screen vibrated again, and I stared at the words, trying to burn through them. I gritted my teeth and punched out my reply. **'I don't care.'**

'I know you do,' she retorted.

I growled at the phone in my hand, my knuckles blanching as I gripped it tighter, wanting it to disintegrate in my palm. I ignored her.

What the hell did Tove Savage know anyway? All she knew was how to pretend I didn't exist when other people were around. All she knew was to make me feel vulnerable and needy around her. All she knew was how to break pieces of me day by day.

I threw the phone on my bed and scrubbed my face with my hands, feeling tension sink in beneath my skin.

My phone vibrated again, the glow lighting up the wall.

'I want to give you your birthday present, let me make it up to you.'

'No thanks.' I blew out a long angry breath. What could she possibly give me that would erase the humiliation of today?

I tried to walk away when Tray and his gang of baboons surrounded me minutes into the lunch break. He called out the usual insults and pushed me around a little, his mates clapping his back as though he'd actually accomplished something. When he pushed me into my locker and my head bounced against the cold metal something snapped. It wasn't aggression or anger, it was the will to fight back. I couldn't be bothered. I was always going to lose, and Tray loved it when I fought back. I could see it in his eyes, they shone like headlights in a drag race tearing through the finish line. The harder I fought, the more satisfaction he got. So I didn't. I slid to the floor and looked at my feet, my hands dangling between my bent knees.

"Get up Freak," he yelled, but I ignored him. "I said, get up."

I dug deeper into myself, finding that place inside where words didn't sting and pain didn't exist. That place where I could pretend I wasn't real and none of this was happening to me, the place I could hide from the angry bitter world outside.

Hands grabbed me and pulled me up. "When I say stand up, you will stand up," He seethed, hissing into my face. His fist connected with my stomach. I wanted to collapse but two pairs of strong hands were holding me up against the lockers.

Tray hit hard, my body screamed with pain, but still, I didn't look at him, didn't fight. He threw a few more punches but when he saw I wasn't going to give him the satisfaction, he nudged for the gorillas on either side of me to let me go. When they released me, I fell to the floor, doubled over, gasping for breath, my innards on fire, strangling me from inside.

A crowd had gathered around us. It was just what the King wanted, an audience, people to perform for, his adoring cheering peasant. Now that he'd noticed them, he was bound to give them a show and I was fucked.

Tray bent down, watching me gasp A menacing smile spread across his face. "You know, you seem a little down today." He scoffed and I heard the sniggers spreading around. "A little bird told me it was your birthday."

A pang of fear shot through me, fear, but also something warm and satisfying. I knew that little bird and I liked that she was talking about me, even if it was to King Douche. I lay there sucking in breath, not looking at Tray, giving him nothing.

"Happy birthday freak," he stretched that last word as though it was snot on his finger that he smeared it on the back of his pants. "This is a very special occasion. We should celebrate. What do you think, boys?"

The group around him murmured agreement. I felt the excitement as it surged from them and rippled among the gathered mob.

Tray stood up again and raised his voice so that it carried down the hall and to the entire gathering. He licked his lips as though he was about to taste something delicious.

"Every birthday deserves a celebration, and every birthday boy deserves a special suit. A birthday suit."

My eyes must have flashed with something, because a demented grin crossed Tray's face. "Let's get him into his suit, boys."

Hands grabbed at me, large heavy hands which ripped at my backpack, and my jacket and shirt. I tried to roll into the fetal position to protect myself, but I was overrun, overwhelmed, and outnumbered. I heard the rip of the fabric as my shirt pulled apart. My hair tore from my scalp, and my zip was undone.

I screamed. It was somewhere between a howl and a shriek, the sound of a wild wounded animal left to die in a dark wood. The sound smashed and bounced against the walls and lockers, travelling through the crowd that stilled as if they had been shot.

The hands fell away from me, the boys took a step back and I rose from the floor. My ripped shirt hung from me like broken wings. Gasps of horror filled the hall as eyes scoured my scarred, broken body. My chest rose and fell, my hair standing wild and dishevelled in every direction.

Cameras flashed around me as the eager and brutal took joy in my misery.

"You're nothing but a wild beast," Tray sneered, but didn't come closer again.

"What the hell is going on?"

"Babe." Tray's face broke into a happy smile and he wrapped his hand around Tove's shoulder.

Tove's eyes found mine and then travelled the length of my damaged body and shredded clothes. Her mouth fell open, her eyes growing wider the longer she looked. "Tray, what the fu—"

"Don't worry about beast boy over here, he's fine."

"Tray I—"

His eyes landed on mine as his mouth slammed over hers, shutting up any further protest. When he pulled away, his mouth curled into a cruel smile as he walked away, yanking her along. Her head swivelled and our eyes locked, mine narrowing, hers apologetic, silent. Tove remained silent. Obedient to her king.

Fuck her.

I gripped the back of my neck and looked to the ceiling, trying to erase the day. Maybe if I gripped or pulled and screamed, I could rip it from my memories, and set it alight.

'**Come to the window.**' My phone flashed.

'**No!**'

'**Please.**' I could almost hear her as she begged me. I knew that sound. It was ingrained into my soul, for she'd begged me so often. For forgiveness, for another chance, for our friendship to remain her dirty little secret.

I exhaled. She knew with that one little word she could twist my inside and make me grovel through a field of glass just to make her happy. I hated that feeling and relished in it. A twisted, sick, love-struck puppy.

I walked over to my window and opened it. She gasped and then smiled. I could feel the warmth of it, the joy she shared with me. She knew how much this meant.

I stared at her, my brows furrowed, my arms folded across my chest. What did she want now?

She stood at her window dressed in a purple shirt with the word 'love' plastered across it. It was too small and hung just above her panties, showing off a sliver of skin. Sweat erupted across my skin, catching a glimpse of her perfectly taut stomach above the lacy underwear.

I swallowed hard, my heart lodging in my throat. She was stunning with her long hair cascading across her shoulders and those piercing blue eyes that burned through me with the blue flicker of their flame.

I could hear my heart in my ears and nothing else. My breath stalled and my heart stumbled as Tove grabbed the hem of her shirt and agonisingly slow pulled it from her body. She let it slip from her hand, her eyes locked on my face as my gaze swept over her glorious body.

She was all breath-taking curves, exposed, vulnerable, exquisite. Her pink nipples pebbled in the cold and all I wanted was to touch them, taste them, feel them. Feel her. My cock came to life, pushing against my jeans. I'd never been so hard, so swollen. My whole body felt taut and stiff. The buzzing of the phone pulled me from my daze.

'Close your mouth before you swallow something.'

I looked at her face. It was red and flushed and her chest rose and fell in shallow breaths. Her hand skimmed her chin. I followed the movement of her hand as it slid down her slender neck. The skin on my face and throat burned, and all I wanted was to reach over and place my hand there, everywhere, to see if her skin was as smooth as it looked.

I cleared my throat and fumbled with my phone. This sucked. I was too far away.

'This is worse.'

Her face fell as she read my message.

'How is this worse?'

'Cause all I want to do is touch you, but you're over
there, and I'm over here.'

Her tongue darted out, flicking over her lower lip, then
she put her phone to her ear. I snatched it midway through
the ring.

I could hear her shallow breath and her voice, unrecognisable and husky. "Does this help?" Her hand slipped up and
cupped her breast, kneading it, rolling her nipple between
her thumb and finger.

My cock throbbed against my jeans, threatening to rip
right through the fabric.

My mouth fell open and I gaped unashamedly as Tove
touched herself in all the ways I wanted to. Her voice pierced
my daze.

"I want you to have a *happy* birthday." Her raspy voice
teased through the receiver. She was so fucking close and so
fucking far away and my mind buzzed with despair. Delight.
A burning, urgent need to have Tove Savage.

I undid my zip and pushed my hand into my pants,
curling cold fingers around my cock.

"Just pretend it's me," she whispered, then let the phone
fall from her hand.

I watched as her hands rolled along her body, her face
flushed, uncertain and brave, stunning in its tentative
boldness.

I gasped at the feel of my hand along my cock as if it was
a foreign hand, as if I hadn't done this a million and one
times in the last three years. I stroked my erection, my eyes
glued on Tove's hard nipples, on her roving hands, on her
parted mouth. My pulse hammered, spreading warmth
through my body as if someone lit a match inside of me,
burning with intense, unrelenting pleasure.

I slicked my hand up and down my hardening shaft, my
grip tightening as I held myself up against the windowsill.

The pressure built inside me and I knew I wouldn't be able to hold on much longer. My ragged breath hitched as I watched Tove slide her hand into her underwear. It was my undoing. I released a choked throaty grunt as my entire body shuddered and I exploded over the windowsill, coming and coming like I had never come before. Ecstasy rolled across my body in unrelenting waves of pleasure.

Tove's face was flushed and her eyes were wide, locked on my cock in my hand. Her mouth hung slightly open, her hand still in her underwear. The image inked itself into my retinas as I found air to refill my lungs. I rolled back against my wall, catching my breath, pulling myself together. Through my daze, I heard my name. It was faint and distant till I remembered my phone. I reached for it, my breath still coming in waves.

"Happy birthday, Adrian," she said in a husky voice.

I shot her a final glance as she turned her lights off.

I cleaned myself up and settled on my bed, my hot body sticking to the cold sheets. I swiped a hand across my face and grabbed the phone, staring at it for what felt like a very long time, then I typed.

'**You need to stop this.**'

'**Stop what?**'

'**This...**'

'**I don't understand.**'

'**I think you do.**'

The screen remained dark. I sucked in a terrified breath when my phone rang, the vibrations shuddering through me. I put it to my ear.

"You didn't like your birthday present?" Her broken voice pierced my silent room and made my chest ache.

I sighed, pinching the bridge of my nose, "No. I mean yes that was.... amazing...but, you can't do that, Tove."

"What?"

"Make me feel like this."

'What? Good?"

"No. Yes." I ground my teeth and groaned. Silence stretched between us as I searched the darkness for the right words.

"You know..." I bit my lower lip and blew out a frayed breath. "You know how I feel about you, Tove, but you and me, we're never going to..."

"Don't say that."

I scoffed. "Don't say what? That you won't ever admit how you really feel about me? That you're happy to keep me hidden away like a dirty little secret? Set aside to be used only when all your *friends* aren't around. You're tearing me apart, Tove."

"I love you." Her words singed the edges of my soul.

"No, you just need me to love you so I can fill the hole in your heart, the one your mum and dad and everyone else left."

"Fuck you, Adrian."

"I think we both know that will never happen."

I heard the gasp on the other end. "Adrian..."

"I can't do this anymore..."

"But you're my best friend."

"Friends? Friends don't do what we just did."

"Adrian..."

"Will you hold my hand at school? Will you tell your 'friends' we're dating? Will you let me kiss you in front of everyone? Will you let me kiss you?"

Her endless heavy silence was all the answer I needed.

"Why can't you see how much you're hurting me? Killing me? Just stop, Tove... Please," I choked out as I heard the quiver of sobs on the line...

"Adrian, don't..."

"I wish..." The words fell from my mouth, crashing to the floor. Wishes don't come true for beasts, for freaks, for the bad guys, so there was no room for wishing here. I let the wish go unfinished, just like our love, our kisses, our words. "If you really want to give me a present from my birthday, just leave me alone..."

"Adrian..."

"Goodnight."

Tove 18

The minutes ticked over slowly. My gaze drifted around the class of half-sleeping students with glazed looks. I glanced over, catching Nikki's eyes. She wiggled her eyebrows and cocked her head towards Tray. She was about as inconspicuous as a fart in a perfume factory.

He'd asked me to the prom just as I knew he would, and for the last two months, all that Nikki and Romy could talk about was how I was finally going to get laid. Neither of them seemed to have any problems when it came to spreading their legs, but for some reason when it came to Tray and me, I always felt a sense of reluctance. Like it should mean something. Like I should be sure. Prom felt like a good time to be sure.

I didn't mind. Sleeping with Tray was an eventuality I always knew would come. He'd been pretty good about the whole thing, considering. We'd been together two and a half years and he'd been more than patient— as he liked to remind me every other day. He'd done just about everything else with my body except stick his dick into it. Either way, getting it over and done with would settle Tray and his urges as he called them.

It's not that I didn't enjoy it when he touched me, and it's not that my body didn't want more. It was just – somewhere, in the deep dark recesses of my mind, there was always another name screaming at me from inside a cell I'd thrown him into. Even though he never touched me, not in that way, whenever I thought about Adrian, a light inside me flickered that made everything feel warm.

Adrian.

After his sixteenth birthday, things haven't been the same between us. We still hung out, but not as much. We still talked, but not as often. For the first time since I met him, he'd flinch away from my touch, as if I was flesh eating bacteria. His smiles looked pained and his eyes were a well of want so deep I wanted to fall into them, but every time I broached the subject he shut down and shut me out, until I stopped trying, or wanting. Until I pretended not being with him, didn't leave me hollow in a way I didn't know I could feel. Adrian should have been my everything but instead, we drifted apart on the same current. The more we paddled towards one another, the farther apart we got.

We let each other drown.

I tried to talk to Adrian about going to prom, but he refused. He'd been acting funny ever since prom came up. I tried to coax him into asking Jane Copeland— a shy little thing with a mousy face and pierced nose. She wore black and her hair was tipped with blue— but he growled and got all antsy about it till I just dropped it.

A few times I thought he might ask me, as if the words were just on the tip of his tongue, and then he'd swallow them as though they never existed. Fuck him, he was the one that pushed me away. He was the one that catapulted me into

Tray's arms. Fuck his longing looks and brooding silences. Fuck Adrian Rose.

Except that if I look hard enough and deep enough, I knew that was all I wanted to do. Fuck Adrian Rose.

My body heated as I thought about it. *Him*. The way his face contorted and his eyes glazed over and his entire body jerked with a grunt that crossed our yards and forced its way right into my heart.

I sighed and rolled my eyes at Nikki, then looked away.

The bell finally rang, and the room sprang up in unison, everyone talking over everyone else, milling like buffalos out of the lecture room. A heavy arm winged my shoulders and the hand slipped down, squeezing my breast.

I pushed Tray's hand away. Ever since we talked about prom night, he'd been more brazen with my body.

"I've told you to stop doing that."

He kissed my neck and his warm breath was in my ear "I can't help it babe, I just want you so badly."

"Not long now." I brushed him off.

"I know." He pulled me into a wet slobbering kiss, his thick tongue crawling into my mouth. "Can't wait." He unlatched himself from me then focused on something behind us.

"Take a picture, freak. It will last longer."

I turned to see Adrian standing in the corner of the room, his eyes glued on us, hooded, angry.

"Leave him alone Tray," I tried.

"Why do you even care about this freak?"

"Tray, just drop it." I sighed, not wanting to go through it all again.

"Fine." Tray hissed through gritted teeth, then pulled me into him, turning my back to Adrian so he could see Tray's hand squeeze my ass, while his mouth was plastered on mine. When Tray felt he'd laid his claim, he ran out of the classroom where his teammates high fived him, giving me knowing looks.

I felt pissed on. I shook the feeling away.

"He's all class," Adrian growled at me.

"Can we not?"

He shrugged. "Whatever."

"Hey," I called to him as he made to leave the room.

He turned to look at me with his intense hungry eyes that made me want to squirm. "Are you coming tonight?"

"No. Have fun." He left without a backwards glance.

⁓⚓

The pounding on the door wrenched me away from the mirror. I took a final look at myself and my heart panged, wishing my mum could be here. Wishing anyone would. My eyes welled with tears and a small flame of anger licked my skin. My dad could have been here to see me off, but as usual, he was on some important business trip. Probably sticking his dick in another intern.

I gulped in a deep breath and fanned my face, willing the threatening tears to go away. It took me an hour to apply my makeup and it looked perfect. I looked perfect in my ridiculously expensive, light aqua mermaid dress. The lace bodice glittered with a sprinkling of sparkles and hugged my frame. The sheer skirt flared out around me. At least daddy was good for something.

I plastered a smile on my face and walked downstairs and through my empty house. Looking straight at the door, I swallowed all my sadness, all my dead hopes and wishes that my parents actually cared.

The banging on the door continued and I swung it open. Tray stood in the doorway, in a black fitted tuxedo, his dirty blond hair slicked back, wearing a grin that told me he was about ready to skip the dancing and everything in between and just get between my legs.

"You look nice," he drawled, and turned away toward the waiting limo, leaving me by my front door. I took a final glance around the house and when I looked down, I found a single red rose, clipped and housed in a clear container, by my feet.

I picked it up and started walking across my yard. Loud music and laughter blared from the limo. My eyes flickered to Adrian's window. And there he was, standing, watching me with that incredibly intense stare of his as if he was seeing everything, not the flesh and bones I was made of, but every emotion and fake smile and self-doubt and stupid regret.

Our eyes locked for a split second and then he melted away into the darkness of his room. I tucked the rose into my hair.

Tray yanked me into the limo where Nikki was sucking face with Rob and Romy was sipping on a can of beer. I knew she hated that stuff, but she was so obsessed with Cullum she would eat shit if he told her to. He was probably the second most popular guy at school which was why Tray and he were so close. They could pass for brothers, tall, bulky and blond, with a take-shit-from-no-one attitude. With their winning streak at the school championships, they ruled the school and got away with pretty much everything, and they knew it. All they had to do was show up for games and win, then, even the faculty pretended that their misadventures didn't happen.

Tray planted a hand over my thigh. It was way too high and my tight dress wasn't giving him the access he was looking for. He grumbled something as the limo took off and handed me some beer. I shook my head. He shrugged and downed it in three long sips, finishing off with an ear-cracking belch.

The boys laughed. The girls giggled. What is it with a few muscles and some testosterone that made us melt and make stupid ass decisions? Who cared? It was prom night. As the limo pulled out in front of the hall, my phone chimed. I grabbed it and looked at the message.

'You look stunning. Have a good night.' My heart chugged for a second, then Tray slung his arm across my shoulder and herded me inside.

The hall was decorated in an ocean theme. Blue curtains hung along the walls. Jellyfish and cardboard fish swung from the ceiling, while fairy lights glowed softly in the dimness. We posed for all the pictures and found our table and got lost in the party.

We danced. I danced. I moved and rolled with the music that thudded and echoed inside the chambers of my body, carrying me with its rhythm. I felt the kind of freedom that skydivers feel as they plummet from a plane towards Earth, heart thudding, endorphins flowing like mad in my veins. I don't know how long I danced before I realised I hadn't seen Tray for a while.

I left the dance floor, sweat peppering my brow, my heart chugging with excitement. I spotted Romy and Cullum exchanging saliva. She was flushed and dazed, and his hands cupped her ass, squeezing as he pulled her closer.

I searched the hall. Tray wasn't there. I burst out into the glaring hallway. The lights harsh after the dimmed party lights. And there they were. The fuckers weren't even hiding, they weren't even trying.

Tray's hand was kneading Nikki's right breast and her hand was deep in his hair, their faces mashed together in a hungry kiss. They looked like two feral animals about to go at it. I stood frozen, my throat closing as I watched. She moaned into his mouth and he pulled into her, hungrier, deprived, crazed.

Disgust rolled through me. I didn't want to look but my

eyes refused to unglue themselves. My throat locked and my chest ached. My lungs burned as though filling up with water. I was drowning. The betrayal sank deep into my bones, turning everything to jelly, dissolving my trust and friendships.

I must have gasped as they both jerked their heads in my direction. We all exchanged a silent stunned look, then Tray shoved Nikki away as if she was infectious. Tray swiped his mouth and came towards me. I bolted, my stupid high heels slowing me down, clinking on the tiled floor.

His hand closed around my elbow and he yanked me back, spinning me so I could face him.

"Tove." His eyes were wild. "It's not what it looks like."

"Let go of me," I wailed, trying to wrench my elbow from his ironclad grip. The more I fought the tighter it got, his thick fingers digging into my skin. "You're hurting me," I cried, but he didn't release me.

"Tove, come back to the party."

"Let me go," I squealed at him. "I won't go anywhere with you, you asshole!"

"Tove, it wouldn't look good if I left here without you."

"Wouldn't look good? How does it look to me when you are playing tonsil hockey with one of my best friends? How about an apology?"

"You're right, I'm really sorry, now come on." He pulled me closer with his firm grip, his head cocked and his lips puckered as if he was going to kiss me.

My stomach rolled and my free hand connected with his face. The sound lost beneath the music leaking in from the party. He released me. Not because I hurt him, but because he was surprised. His hand shot to his face and his eyes clouded over.

"Bitch!"

But I was already running again. The door was right there.

One.

More.

Step.

Tray's hands landed on my shoulders and I came to an abrupt halt, my head whipping backwards as though I'd just run into a brick wall. His hands slipped over my dress, reaching for my breasts. His hot breath on my ear.

"I'm sorry, Tove, I'm just a little drunk. Come back to the party with me." His voice was warm and husky and his hands firm, as they roamed my torso.

I pushed away from him and turned to face him. He swiped away an errant hair and smiled at me.

"Come on, Tove, it was just a little kiss. It won't happen again."

My whole body burned with fury, like a slithering beast that spread under my flesh. I gritted my teeth, holding back all my pain and devastation. I wasn't going to give him that satisfaction.

Cullum appeared from somewhere and I spotted Nikki and Romy whispering at the end of the hall. Nikki's eyes met mine and I could see the regret, but I didn't care, she'd sliced me open right to the core.

"I am going home." My voice came out in a pathetic whisper.

Tray groaned his frustration and Cullum splayed a hand on his chest, stopping any further advance towards me. "Let her go, man. Nikki clearly doesn't mind sharing." He chuckled and pushed against Tray.

He stood there, eyes locked on mine. "Tove…"

I turned away and stepped outside. The autumn air was chilly, and I gulped it into my burning lungs. My whole body shook, and I bit my lower lip, holding the tears that threatened to fall.

I called an Uber. When it arrived, I rushed inside, slamming the door in my wake. I stared out the window, avoiding my own reflection, my stupidity staring back at me. My phone chimed and beeped, message after message. I didn't look. I knew who they were from. I knew what they would say.

The Uber pulled up at my house and my eye automatically flicked to Adrian's window. His light was on.

I ran up to my room and fell into my bed, misery swaddling me like a wet cloth.

My phone chimed. And my eyes fell to the message.

'You're home early.'

I didn't reply. It chimed a second time.

'Did you have fun?'

I didn't answer. I couldn't bring myself to do it.

'Are you okay?'

I bit my lower lip and curled up on the bed, the tears hanging on the edge of my irises.

'Can you come over?'

'That's not a good idea.'

'Please.' I let the phone fall from my hand and waited. I hadn't asked anything of him for so long. I heard the front door open and shut and the third step creaked as Adrian made his way to me.

I could feel him. There was something about the way he filled a room. While all the other boys filled out, he stayed this ropey skinny thing with long arms and stick legs, and the most beautiful fucking face I've ever seen. Unevenly beautiful, carved in half. Maybe it wasn't that he was big and strong but the way he made me feel when he was near me. Safe, warm, complete.

"Tove? Are you okay?"

"No." I whimpered and then my barriers broke and the tears came. Adrian was by my side in seconds, sitting on the edge of the bed, coaxing my head onto his lap. He stroked my cheek while I cried, heaving ugly tears.

"What happened Tove? Are you hurt? Tove?"

I was trapped in my stupid dress with its tight skirt and puffy frills at the bottom, like an overgrown dried up mermaid. My makeup ran onto his saturated jeans, but Adrian didn't flinch or try to wipe the tears away. He didn't say a word. He let me cry until I had no more tears.

I lay there, dazed and drained. Adrian got up and opened my top drawer, pulling out a T-shirt.

"Let's get you out of this dress so you can rest." His face was creased with worry, but he didn't push or nudge. He waited. Adrian always waited. For me.

I lifted myself from the bed and turned my back to him, grabbing the side zipper. I pulled at the stupid thing, but it didn't release, I pulled and yanked till more tears came. I couldn't even take my bloody dress off.

His hand covered mine, warm and calm. He waited. I moved my hand away while lifting the other, tucking it over my head. Adrian clasped the zipper. Ever so slowly, he released the fabric, his knuckles trailing my skin as he unzipped the dress, leaving a scorching trail in his wake.

The dress fell from my body and I stepped out of it. My back still to Adrian, who discarded it somewhere. From behind me he passed me my shirt. I took it from him, the limp thing hanging in my hand, then, without thinking, I let it drop, and turned to face Adrian.

His mouth fell open and his throat bobbed as I took a step closer to him, then another, wrapping my hands around his neck.

His forehead leaned into mine and our breath mingled.

"Tove?" It was a question that demanded an answer.

I brushed my lips with his, a fiery trail of want spreading through my body. His hand reached for my hair and pulled out the tiara, like a broken crown on my broken throne. He threw it on the floor, his eyes locked with mine as he tugged out clip after clip, his fingers dancing around my scalp, releasing my hair. With a final pull, it cascaded along my back, and his hand caught the rose and handed it to me.

His hand plunged into my loose hair and his fist wrapped around the fallen locks. He tugged, forcing my head up, and then the boy I thought I knew disappeared before my eyes.

Adrian's mouth crashed against mine, capturing me in a long burning kiss. He wasn't forceful or sloppy, but soft and warm, hungry to explore my mouth, just as hungry as I was for his. He groaned and his fist tightened around my hair. My tongue swept past his lips and I felt his entire body shudder against me, as we both searched for something more.

We pulled apart and he sucked in a frayed breath, his hand still in my hair, his face a mask of confusion and desire. "Tove, do you want this?"

I pushed away from him, set the rose on my desk and lay down on my bed. Heat spread through me as his eyes roamed across my body. "I want this Adrian, you, I want you."

With that all his reluctance fell away and he prowled closer to the bed, shedding his shirt, and undoing his pants. I took in his torso, the wiry boy, made of muscle and skin and scarred from top to bottom. Long scars marked his pale skin.

He stalked onto the bed and his mouth found mine, no longer soft, no longer kind but heated and frenzied and desperate as if I had unleashed a beast kept too long in captivity. His warm mouth sucked mine, as he drew my lips between his teeth. His hand found my breast and he groaned with haunted desperation as his warm fingers traced the swollen outline until he found a nipple.

His mouth unlatched from mine. Adrian peppered kisses along my neck, down my collar bone. Working his way down.

I knew it was coming and yet when his hot mouth closed around my nipple my mind reeled with the pleasure of it. I shuddered against him as he explored the edges of my sanity, sucking and biting, tugging and teasing my aching nipples, devouring them like he was a man on death row and I was his last meal.

Adrian took his time, savouring each flick and swirl of his tongue until I thought I might explode, my thighs squeezing tightly together. "Adrian." It was a breathy desperate whisper which he ignored, going to work on the other side, his lips and teeth grazing my flushed skin.

Adrian traced an unbearably slow line from my nipple to the band of my underwear. "Tell me to stop, Tove," he whispered against my skin, his gravelly voice hoarse, raw.

My silent reply hung between us.

Adrian's finger crept into my underwear until he found my warm wet pussy. We both gasped, both froze, both felt the pulse of that moment as it smashed against us in that room. We had crossed a line, one that we could never uncross.

"Fuck, Tove," he whispered against my navel as he slipped my underwear off, kissing every inch of my skin, his hands, his eyes, his tongue, not leaving me for a second. The more he took, the more he gave, all his attention was focused solely on me. He kissed the length of my thighs and I parted them for him in silent approval, desire, invitation.

His head sank between my legs and his tongue darted out and flicked my pussy. I didn't mean to whimper, but that single flick ignited something in me, more primal, more savage than I had ever experienced. Even after two years with Tray, I had never felt unleashed.

His tongue explored my pussy like a long-lost traveller searching for new lands. As he had with my nipples, he launched a delicate assault, his tongue a deadly weapon that broke me down. My thighs shook and my core coiled, my body knowing what it needed and what it wanted. My hips ground against his mouth in violent desperate movements. A foreign reckless keening sound erupted from my mouth as I threw my head back, biting onto my forearm. My entire body lit with pleasure so intense I thought I might pass out.

I lay on my bed, embarrassed, elated, flushed and shattered.

"Fuck, Tove," Adrian kissed my navel, and nipples as he made his way back up to my face. "That was amazing,"

He kissed me gently and I could taste myself on him, the delicacy he so eagerly enjoyed. I pulled myself closer to him and sank my hand into his boxers. He gasped and grabbed my wrist.

"Tove…"

"It's your turn."

"Tove, I…"

"Shhh – I want this." I rolled over him and reached over to my bedside table, pulled out the drawer, and felt for the strip of condoms. I flicked a foil to Adrian, his eyes flitting from me to the condom.

I found his mouth, sucking on his plump lips, swollen and hot from their hard work. I kissed his long neck and rolled my tongue along the long-twisted scar that ran over his shoulder and all the way to his right nipple. My teeth grazed his nipple and he drew in a sharp breath.

I licked the scar that ran from his navel across his hip bone which stuck out from his wiry frame. I pulled off his boxers and could feel him tense. His hard cock pulsed, an angry vein throbbing along his massive erection. He grabbed my wrist as I tried to curl my fingers around it.

"If you touch it, I'll be done." He bit his lip and his jaw twitched.

"Okay." I lay on my back, allowing him to sit up and work the condom out.

Adrian blanketed me with his body, his eyes pinning me in place. I felt the tremble in his hands, the tension inside of him as his neck corded. Then he asked one last time.

"Do you want this, Tove?" His cock pushed against my

entry and all I wanted was to know what Adrian Rose felt like inside me.

"I want this Adrian. I want you." It sounded like a cry, and he leaned his forehead against mine for a second before he started pushing awkwardly against me, slipping around.

"Let me." I grabbed his cock and he shuddered as my fingers curled around him. I was amazed at the size of it, of him. I bit my lower lip and guided him. "There."

He looked at me again with that torn expression, the one that questioned my motives, the one that knew there was more to this than just wanting him. But I didn't want to think about the truth then. I just wanted to feel Adrian, to be with Adrian. I'd let him love me as only he could, and so I pushed against him, the head of his cock slipped inside me and I felt *everything*.

The electric tingle of my nerves, the shortness of my breath, the tension in my lungs and all my muscles clenched and tightened around him, in shock, in invitation, in fear, in want. His eyes were wide and his breath hitched as inch by inch he slid inside me.

He settled there just for a moment, deep inside me. We were one being, fused flesh and breath and heat. Adrian started moving, his body covered in sweat, his face drenched in awe and desperate desire.

He pecked my lips, but it was as if he couldn't concentrate. As if he wanted all of me at once but couldn't get everywhere. Instead, his cock started moving faster inside me and his face contorted in anguished delight. He was gasping, a desperate grunt that warped his face. The scar pulled the skin in every direction, forcing his lips to snarl and his furrowed head to wrinkle and he looked like a beast as he groaned desperately, clutching the sheet by my head, his knuckles so white they dissolved into the linen.

"Tove!" It sounded like a desperate cry. Adrian pounded himself brutally inside me, frenzied and feverish, his face tormented, his eyes clenched shut. He clutched my shoulders, his body jerked, his cock sank into me, ever deeper, drawing me closer, burying himself inside as if he could never be deep enough. His forehead fell against my chest, and his ragged breath heated my breasts as we pulled ourselves together.

He rolled away, and his eyes couldn't seem to find mine.

"Did I hurt you?" He sounded fearful, uncertain.

"A good hurt," I said and I meant it. My pussy throbbed, my body missing his. "That was…" and I had no words, because *amazing* and *special* sound so dull, so muted compared to what we just did together.

"Tove…" I heard all his feelings on the edge of his voice, like a familiar song and I prayed he wouldn't say the words I know he'd been aching to say to me for eight years, the words that would tear us apart, words that would shatter everything. "Are you okay?"

Our eyes met and I knew what he was really asking. I smiled thinly, knowing this would all end soon. "I am now." I pulled him to me and kissed him gently, my lips grazing his.

"Tove." His raspy voice was anguished, "I've wanted this for so long…"

"I know, I've wanted it too…"

"But…?"

"I'm with Tray."

He pulled away from me, anger flaring in his eyes.

"If you're with Tray, what are you doing here, with me?"

I bit the inside of my cheek, a sinking feeling washing over me. "Adrian –" I reached for him, but he flinched away, his face twisted.

"Tell me what happened." His voice was no longer kind, no longer soft.

As I spoke, I saw his entire body shift and change, growing stiffer. His shoulders straightened, his mouth thinned and his stunning green eyes darkened with anger.

"Tray is such a fucking douche."

"Don't say that."

"You're defending him?"

"He was drunk. He didn't mean it."

"Tove –" He wrenched a hand through his hair and his face crumpled.

"Don't, Adrian…"

"Don't?" Lightning struck in the forest of his eyes. "What was all this then? You used me to get back at him?"

"It's not like that."

"Isn't it?" His nose flared and his eyes grew wider. "Then leave him, be with me. I know you want to…that's the way it should be!" His bare chest rose and fell, and I traced the scars with my gaze, unable to meet his.

A heavy silence filled the room, it bore down on us, suffocating.

"Tove?" His voice was clipped, edged with hope. But when I looked to his face, I saw he knew.

He bolted from the bed as if it was suddenly on fire, and grabbed his pants, slamming his legs into them.

"Adrian." He ignored me as he searched for his discarded shirt.

"Adrian." I was out of my bed, reaching for him.

"Don't touch me." He hissed and flinched away from my touch as if I'd just burned him.

"Adrian don't…"

"Don't?" he screamed, his face twisted. "Don't? You just… we just… and now you're going to go back to that cheating fucker?" His hand sliced the air in wild movements.

"You're acting like a wild animal. A beast."

"I. Am. Being. A. Beast?" he spoke slowly, drawing each word out, his chest heaving as he stalked towards me, pinning me to my wall, his face contorted. "Tray is a fucking loser and all he wants is to stick his dick in you. He will never love you, never respect you, and never really know you."

"You don't know Tray."

"Oh, I know him very well and it seems, so does Nikki."

"Fuck you, Adrian."

"You already have." He panted and snarled, his chest rising with heavy breaths, his shoulders hunched above me, every muscle in his body taut and stretched, every bit the beast I've made him out to be. His wild eyes roamed my naked body, still on display for him.

"Well clearly that was a mistake."

He baulked like I'd bitten him.

I watched him collapse like a tower of dominoes imploding in on itself. It was quick and brutal and agonising and all I wanted was to reach out to him and comfort him. Instead, I let him go.

He turned away from me, found his shirt and slipped it back on.

His gaze locked on my face, and inside the forest of his eyes I saw the broken, cracked bark and fallen leaves, all the pain and disbelief crashing from him. Then he marched out of my room, a silent ugly escape that left in its wake a void so deep I feared I might fall and never find a way out. I backed away and onto my bed as if it was a safe haven.

I fell on my back, tears pooling in my eyes as I stared at the ceiling, the sensation of elation seeping away, leaving me in a pool of regret. I didn't regret sleeping with Adrian. I loved him so much it hurt to think about. I loved him so much his touch burned itself under my skin. I loved him so much that breaking him was better than letting myself break.

No, I didn't regret sleeping with him, but I did regret using him as a balm, as a fucked-up patch-up job for my broken heart and wounded ego. I'd used his kindness and willingness to try and erase Tray's betrayal from me, but even as I lay there, the sweat which smelt of Adrian's sex and heat and body cooling on my body, I was already reaching for my phone.

My hand brushed the rose he'd given me. My fingers curled around the delicate leaves, closing crushing, gripping until the petals bruised and crumbled and fell like tears to the floor.

⚜

Adrian

I replayed the last two hours in my head over and over again. The whole thing felt like a wet dream, one that I'd lived and fantasised about in my head since my first hard on. Since I first started noticing Tove as more than just a friend that was a girl, but as a girl that was a *girl*.

I tasted her every time I licked my lips, and it reminded me of the watermelon that glazed my lips after our first kiss. Every time I thought about her creamy breasts and her tight wet pussy, my cock pushed and throbbed against my pants. And every time I thought about her words, it shrivelled up and hid under my curly pubic hair.

My whole body clenched at the thought of Tove, my stomach, my jaw, my fists, my heart. I was torn to pieces, desire and hatred mixed to create a noxious angry concoction that I swallowed and wallowed in like a pathetic creature. A beast. She had poisoned me, cursed me, and I would forever carry the mark with me. It was a slash so deep and savage that it would never heal, and never stop hurting. It would never scab over, but always remain bleeding and agonising.

I pounded my fists against my mattress and growled into my pillow. If she wanted a beast, I would give her one.

When I woke up on Saturday morning, Tove's sex smell still lingered on my sweaty body. Showering felt good.

Showering was washing her away, her touch, her moans, her fucking choices. There would be no more Tove Savage, I would rip her memories from my heart and move on.

I walked into my room, a towel wrapped around my waist, and there she was in her window looking right at me. Her face lit up and she flashed me a smile. I marched over to the window and swiped the curtain shut, my heart slamming like an ice pick against an iceberg.

My phone chirped. I glanced at the words on the screen.

'I'm sorry.'

I let the words hang on the screen like dead men hanging from their nooses. I threw my towel on the floor and got dressed just as my phone chirped a second time.

'Come to the window.'

I wrenched a hand through my hair and stared at the words. I left the phone on my bed and slipped a shirt over my head.

The phone chirped a third time.

'Adrian, come on, talk to me.'

I scoffed at the text. *'Talk to me.'* I ignored it and went on with my day. There was nothing left to talk about.

The weekend passed like a long fart, it stank and hung around heavy to breathe in and unavoidable in cramped spaces.

I skulked through the halls on Monday morning, wishing I was invisible. There were two weeks left of school and I could taste the freedom they would afford me. I could get the fuck out of Dodge. If Tove hadn't been so desperately trying to get back at Tray, maybe I would have had a chance to tell her I got a scholarship on the West Coast. Until Friday, I had planned to stay for the summer, and get my fill of sunshine and Tove, but now I just wanted to get out, and away. I could find a job around campus and fuck every freshman I met till I fucked Tove Savage out of my system.

Avoiding Tove should have been the easiest thing in the world. I spent so much time trying to be around her that I knew her schedule, where she hung out during lunch breaks and where she would be after school. I knew where Tove was going to be every minute of every day, and anywhere she was, I wasn't.

Or that was the plan.

She was meant to be in the gymnasium, for sports class. I stalled as I saw her down the hall, King Douche's hand wrapped around her shoulder like he fucking owned her. She had a long streak of black eyeliner that made her blue eyes feline-like and vicious. She looked fucking stunning in a cut off pink top and short shorts that barely covered her ass. Her ass. Round and perfect like the rest of her.

I tried not to think about it as I took a galvanising breath and marched on. I should have turned around. I should have taken the stairs to the first floor and walked the long way around. I should have done so many things.

"Look who it is." Tray spun around, taking Tove in his wake and stepped in my way. "Why, it is the hunchback of Notre Dame."

Tove's eyes shot to mine but she said nothing. I gritted my teeth.

"Aren't you going to say anything, Pinocchio?"

I tried to sidestep Tray, but Cullum blocked my way, an immovable mountain.

"What's wrong, Rumpelstiltskin, cat got your tongue?"

I sighed and met his gaze with a cold stare. "It's Quasimodo."

Tray pushed Tove away and grabbed the collar of my T-shirt. I didn't fight as he slammed me against the wall, my breath coming out in a violent thud while his was warm on my face. "What the fuck did you just call me?"

"The hunchback of Notre Dame. His name was Quasimodo," I deadpanned.

He smirked at me and slammed my back into the wall again.

"You think you're funny, *freak?*"

"What I think is funny, is that I was inside your girlfriend three nights ago."

"What the fuck did you just say?" he growled through an iron jaw.

"Ask her." I smirked.

His head whiplashed from Tove to me, her eyes slits.

"Tove, what the fuck is he talking about?"

I sucked in a long deep breath. This was it, I would force her to choose, to tell the truth, to spill our ugly secret and show it to the world where is could glow and grow and live.

"I don't fucking know, I mean look at him, you think I'd let that thing near me?"

The three boys burst into mad laughter and my eyes burned into Tove's which were glistening with tears.

Shame?

Anger?

Or maybe they were pity?

She should have been crying for the death of our friendship. She had just thrown the last of the gravel on the grave and buried it.

"Liar," I snapped at her.

Tray ploughed my body into the wall, but I no longer cared. My heartstrings tore apart, shredded, hanging by a loose thread still tethered to Tove. "Stop talking, freak," he snarled, his nostrils flaring, his eyes manic.

"Leave him alone." Tove's voice sliced the ugly tension between us.

Tray laughed at her.

"There she is again, your knight in shining armour. When are you going to grow a pair and stick up for yourself freak? Why does my girlfriend have to stand up for you all the time?'

"Why don't you ask her?" I smirked at him. "Then again, I do know her better than you… in fact, while you got to stick your tongue down Nikki's throat, I got to dip mine inside her pu—"

Turned out that was the wrong answer as next thing I knew his fist connected with my head. I ricocheted backwards into the wall and the world exploded behind my eyes. I could hear shouting or maybe screaming. It didn't matter, all I could feel was pain. Hot searing pain that spread around my body like a balm. I held onto the pain, the sheer intensity of the agony. It made it so I didn't have to think about all the other pain, the stuff inside, that bleeding slash still spewing endless blood and tears.

I felt weightless, but it was probably when Tray released me and I slid along the wall. My hand ran over my face and I felt the hot blood as it spewed down my face, coating my shirt and cheek and chin. It tasted like metal and anger and hatred.

"That's going to leave a mark," Tray's voice joked as silence descended in the hall.

I clenched my fists, my nails digging into my palm. The pain soothed the rage and anguish.

"Oh, my God, Adrian, are you okay?"

It was Mrs Robinson, my English teacher. She'd always had a soft spot for me, or maybe it was for my dad.

Sixteen fucking stitches and another scar. Dad kept stealing glances at me as we drove home in silence. I bolted out of the car the minute he pulled up to the driveway and slammed the door to my room. I gave him an out, took the pressure off. We didn't have to talk about it. We didn't have to talk about anything. We didn't have to talk at all, we didn't know how to anyway.

I spent the last ten days of high school, mostly sneaking around like a thief or hiding like a coward. I just needed to survive. And I did. Barely.

My heart still beat but it was a dying black coal, remnants of the flaming thing it once was.

Tove called almost seventy times and left a score of messages. But all I could see was her face when she sneered. Like a beast. How could I have got it so wrong? So twisted? How did I never see that she was always the monster?

Tove

I hate the city apartment. It's small and cramped and even though it's in an up and coming neighbourhood I hate it. There's never any parking and the street always smells like days old fried food.

I walk towards the elevator and see the sign in crude handwriting which announces that it's out of order. Of course. I rub my eyes and haul my photography gear on my back, regretting not leaving it in the studio. Normally I would, but I wanted to sleep in, maybe even get a snuggle with Tray in the morning. In the last few months it's like we've barely seen one another.

As I climb the stairs I promise myself to try and make more of an effort to see my boyfriend, maybe even get laid. Since when has life got in the way of getting naked with Tray? Between the late nights and early mornings, my late-night shoots and his study groups.

Breathless, I reach the fifth floor and walk towards the door. My clothes stick to my body and sweat drips down my back. I cringe as I stick the key into the door. I want a shower. My mind drifts. I could invite Tray to join me. My thighs clench together at the thought of all the possibilities. I bite my lip and push the door open, stepping inside.

The apartment feels like an oven, everything is too hot. I throw my keys on the dining room table, where Tray's books lie open across it, highlighted sections glaring back at me from the white pages. His LSATs are next week. Finally. Then maybe life can get back to normal.

I put my gear down on the couch and enter the small kitchenette. He hasn't made any dinner. I sigh, irritation tingling against my skin. We've already agreed that as long as he sits at home and studies every day, he will help more around here, while I earn a fucking living and my dad pays his tuition.

Just as I was about to call his name, I hear it. A soft, unmistakable giggle. I freeze and listen. A second giggle, followed by a hungry moan.

What. The. Fuck?

I walk to our bedroom and stand outside. Surely not. This could not possibly be happening to me. Again. My mind drifts for a second, to a skinny scarred boy who lived next door and I shake the memory away. I haven't thought about Adrian in years. Well that's not really true, I think about him almost every day. I bat the thought of him away like a fly and listen.

The moan comes again, huskier this time, hungrier. I push the door open, and there he is, his face between some girl's legs. She whimpers and arches her back.

I stand there like an idiot, watching. My eyes glued to his face between her legs, to her tits jumping up and down every time she wiggles under his touch. I stand there feeling like a fucking idiot, feeling eighteen all over again, prom night all over again, but this time, there is no Adrian to comfort me. There is no one.

My feet feel too heavy to move, my whole body a solid

tree trunk, unmovable, as if I've grown roots. And then her eyes flick open and she gasps. As usual, Tray misinterprets the signals and takes it for encouragement, flicking out his tongue and increasing his pace.

"Stop," she screams and slams her thighs together, scrambling up the bed.

Tray grunts – "what the fuck Eva…" His voice drops off as he swivels his head to follow her gaze and his eyes lock on mine.

In a flash he is up, and his hard cock is like the slap in the face I need to unglue me form the floor. I turn, walk out of the room, and he follows me out, his cock slapping against his flat stomach.

"Tove! Babe."

"Don't." I flinch away. His naked body covered in a layer of perspiration that glints in the glaring lights.

"It's not what it looks like…"

I turn to look at him, anger steaming from me like hot sewage. "Tell me what it looks like Tray, cause from where I am standing, it looks like you were sucking some other girl's pussy in *our* bed."

"Babe…"

"Don't!" I throw my arms up in the air as he slams his legs through his underpants.

I have so many questions running through my head, the knife sinking so deep, my stupidity covering me like a fresh blanket of snow. I am such an idiot. I want to scream at him, to hit him, to ask how long and with how many, but I know everything he'll tell me will be a lie. It's always been, and I've always allowed it, for so many stupid reasons. No more.

"Tove, baby, I can explain…"

"Shut up, Tray." I turn to the kitchen table and grab my keys, marching to the door, because if I look at him again, I might stab him. "I'm going out for thirty minutes, and when I come back, you and the skank need to be out of here."

"Where should I go?'

"I don't give a shit, Tray, just don't be here!" I slam the door as I leave the apartment, feeling the tears brimming behind my lids.

I lean against the peeling yellow wall and try to remember how to breathe. The hallway feels too silent. Did every fucking neighbour just hear my humiliation? Did all of them already know? I run downstairs and get into my car and batter my fists against the steering wheel. Again, and again and again.

I feel like a total idiot. I feel eighteen again and vulnerable and exposed in the worst possible way. The water rises in my throat again and I want to choke on my own pathetic misery.

I shake my head, trying to push away the rising tide, it's familiar and salty and it burns all the wounds which just tore open in my heart. I knew what Tray was like. I've always known, but I always hoped he'd change.

Regret burns through me because I know what I gave up to be with that douchebag.

King Douche.

The name makes my lips twitch in a smile that curdles. The pain of the memory burns deeper and harder than all the other small cuts Tray has placed on my heart. This one hurts most because I caused it. It's the one that's never healed. The one I let go. The one I should have held on to.

Fuck it.

My head swims with too many thoughts, too many wrong fucking decisions, but I am going to start correcting them. Every single one. Starting now. Or starting in the morning.

My nerves are shot and my heart smashed to pathetic little pieces. I need alcohol, and a quick trip to the bottle shop should give Tray and his skank enough time to vacate my fucking apartment.

I put the car into gear and take off, with hardly a noise in my wake, as if I don't even exist.

I play with the radio. Some familiar rock tune comes on and I turn the volume up to full blast. The bottle shop comes into view on my left, but suddenly I don't want to just get a bottle and go home so I drive past it. There's another one, just ten miles up the road. Distance equates to time, and the longer my trip, the more unlikely I am to run into them. I shiver and my skin crawls at the thought of them. *Them.* Bile claws its way up my throat.

I park and sit in the car, staring at the glaring neon sign. Alcohol will help wash away these feelings, the shame and humiliation. Fuck Tray. Fuck everything. A sense of calm passes over me as I feel relieved with my decision. I don't even feel bad.

The young clerk is tall and his dark suspicious gaze follows me around the shop. I would have followed me too. I look like a deranged homeless woman in my too big jumper that falls almost to my knees and swallows my entire figure up. My hair hangs limp like my heart and my face is streaked with mascara. I look like a warrior, not one that's just conquered and won a war, but a defeated broken soldier that's just crawled out of a pit.

I grab a bottle of merlot and make my way to the spirit shelves, grabbing a bottle of vodka.

I almost fall over as I place the bottles on the counter. The clerk rings everything up and I dig for my credit card from the depths of my bag. I feel him judging me. I am deranged and pathetic.

I sigh as he returns my card. I snatch it from him, wishing I could just disappear. I catch the hint of a smile on his face as I grab my bottles.

"Have a good night." His voice mocks me.

I give him a wan smile and run out. I should have given him the finger.

I throw the bottles on the passenger seat as I slide into the driver's seat, slam the key into the ignition and drive out of the parking lot like the deranged woman I am.

I don't know why that little smirk got to me so much. Is it just a culmination of the last five years of my life written across a stranger's face?

You're pitiful.

And I am.

I don't know what distracted me. The radio, or maybe looking through the road but suddenly everything slows down. The blarring horn becomes a distant humming sound drowned by the radio, the DJ's laughter all encompassing. He's laughing at me as the world turns upside down. My face smashes against a window. My nose explodes. Glass flies everywhere. The two bottles pass over my head in a demented dance shattering against one another, the red spilling its guts like a slain deer and mixing with the vodka.

The world feels upside down. And then the car hits the ground with an earth-shattering crunch. The metal buckles and screams. The car slides along the ground, sending up sparks. Metal screeches against tar like fingernails on a blackboard.

My body jerks, then the safety belt yanks me back and I feel a rib shatter. The airbag inflates. There's heat and pain and a terrible stench. And then - there's only darkness.

Tove

"What's the last thing you remember?"

That's an odd question, although he might have asked it already. Or not. I can't remember.

Somewhere behind his deep voice is an incessant beeping, like a fly trying to get out of a room, constantly crashing against the windowpane.

Buzz,

crash,

buzz,

crash,

beep,

beep,

beep.

My head hurts. Everything hurts. I try to open my eyes but they feel as if they have been glued shut. They're too heavy. I am tired. So tired.

I try to open my mouth, but it feels as if it has been stuffed with cotton balls. I stay still and listen. Beyond the white noise and beeping there is that voice again. "Do you know where you are? Do you know what happened to you?"

"Why are you talking to her? She can't hear you." Another voice.

But I can hear. *I can hear* – I scream in my head. Why is nothing working?

I try to force my ears to listen. I try to get my brain to make sense. They sound dim as if I'm wrapped in bubble wrap. Everything dulls and gradually falls away. I try to hang on, grasping at snippets of words.

Don't know.

Not sure when.

Damage.

It's unclear.

Wake up.

Might never.

Why are none of the words making sense? My brain feels fuzzy. My dark world becomes darker.

And then there is nothing.

⁓⋅⚙

Adrian

I can't fucking believe it.

I watch the wounded creature on the bed in front of me and suddenly my stomach knits and my entire body shivers and I don't know if I'm about to vomit or erupt in manic laughter.

Tove.

Tove fucking Savage is here.

In my hospital. Lying like a broken thing under the crisp white sheet. There are far too many machines keeping her alive and everything about her is broken and swollen. I probably wouldn't have recognised her if it wasn't for the name.

In my twenty-two years, I've never heard of another Tove Savage. So, when I read her name in the nurse's station I had to come and see for myself.

It's hard to tell through the swollen shut eyes and shaved hair where they stapled her skull back together, but it is definitely her.

I grab her chart and read over the damage. She's going to be here a while, and I am going to make sure her stay is going to be hell.

I put her chart back, my body expanding with joy.

Revenge is a bitch and my bitch just got handed to me on a hospital gurney.

Tove

The beeping has eased. It's still there, in the background, insistent like a beating heart, but the noise has grown softer, dimmer.

I might have groaned because there's a voice.

"She's awake."

Things hurt.

I do a mental check of my body, yes, every single body part hurts, even my teeth. My head feels as if it's being drilled, the pain is hard and hollow.

I open my eyes. White light floods behind my retinas, burning them like bleach. I moan, and my head lolls back with the pain. I try again, blink a few times and the whiteness saturates, allowing colours to fill my vision.

Eyes.

Three pairs of eyes look down at me, foreheads in deep frowns, stares scrutinising. I suddenly want to disappear.

The older one starts. "Hi, Tove, do you know where you are?"

Tove. That's a strange word. Name. My name. It's *my* name. The occurrence is an odd sensation. Why was that not obvious in the first place?

I squint at the older man, his thick white eyebrows falling like willow leaves over his grey eyes.

I open my mouth.

Pain.

I breathe, regret it. I try again. Words are jammed in my throat, trying to push their way out, but it feels swollen, closed, they crowd behind the skin, choking me. I shake my head. That will have to do.

"You're in the hospital, Tove." The man tries for a smile, but it is weak and sad and it scares me. "My name is Doctor Jäger."

My eyes flicker to the three faces standing around me. A fog clouds my mind and all I feel is helpless. I turn my head and take in my surroundings. I'm lying in a bed. My body feels fuzzy, sore, almost detached. A number of machines surround the bed, and an assortment of plastic tubes find their way into my veins.

"Do you know what happened to you?" The doctor's face stretches into an uncertain expression.

I shake my head as I try to think. What the hell happened? What's the last thing I remember?

I hit a wall. Emptiness. Nothing.

The doctor spoke again. "What's the last thing you remember?"

I notice the younger man flinch at the question, and his brow knits in a severe expression. I search the recesses of my mind, but all I find is blank, empty space.

I shake my head. It feels so fucking heavy. Everything feels heavy, like I'm being pumped full of lead. My eyelids threaten to close.

"Do you remember anything at all?"

I search again, pushing through the fog. I shake my head again.

The doctor nods and crosses his arms across his chest. "You've suffered serious head and back injuries, we had to put you in an induced coma to help your body deal with the swelling around your brain."

I just lie there, letting all the words fall over me like rain. Some sink in, while some slide right off my skin.

I whimper. The man's frown deepens. "It is not uncommon to feel confused and disoriented after a trauma such as the one you experienced." He gives me another of his weak smiles. "You look tired and we may have overwhelmed you already. I'll be back to check on you tomorrow. Gloria over here will take care of you today."

All I can do is lie there. Paralysed by pain and fear and confusion, unable to process, unable to think.

"Get some rest, Tove." A deep smooth voice washes over me. "I'll be here to help you when you wake up."

More beeping, more relief. More darkness.

⁂

Days blur into nights blur into hours and minutes that pass in changed bandages and agonised moans. I am living in the dark. Parts of my body and mind are completely inaccessible. It is infuriating, frustrating, but most of all, petrifying.

I am living in a dream state. Reality merges into dreams. This place has no sense of time. Not really. The medication lulls me into long heavy slumbers where dreams and reality are so vivid, I can't distinguish one from the next. Nothing sinks in. Nothing makes sense.

They are always asking questions, giving me weak smiles, telling me everything is going to be okay.

I don't feel okay. All I feel is pain and alone.

The nurse pulls the curtain open and light floods into the room.

"Good morning Tove, how are you today?" Her beautiful dark voice carries like a song. I've seen her. I want to know her name but it keeps slipping away from me.

"Okay," I manage, my throat feeling dry and ragged.

"Doctor Jäger will be here momentarily, to take you through your treatment plan."

I nod, trying to etch the name into my brain.

"Good morning Tove." A jovial man walks into the room. He feels familiar, like a dream. His eyebrows remind me of willows in the snow. "How do you feel this morning?"

"Okay," I lie.

"Do you remember my name?"

I nod, searching for it in the fog.

"Good. And do you remember where you are?"

"Yes." At least I have one answer for him.

"Wonderful." He beams at me and I think he might pull out a lollipop from his pocket and hand it to me. "Okay, now for some more difficult questions."

I wait.

"Do you know what day it is?"

I bite my lower lip, trying to work out an impossible equation.

"No." My voice quivers a little.

"That's okay. It's Monday. The 28th of February."

I stare at the doctor by my bedside. What does he want me to say?

"Do you remember what happened?"

I wince, trying to find all the information. I know we've had this conversation before, but all the words keep falling away like sand from a sieve.

"I was in an accident?"

"That's right." The doctor smiles then reins himself in. "Do you remember what happened to you?"

"I'm broken." My voice quivers and a big fat tear rolls down my cheek, leaving a hot trail behind it.

The doctor's face softens. "Tove. I know how hard this must be for you, but there is good news." He tries for his smiles again. "You had the best surgeons work on your compression fracture and in time your back will heal, and you will walk out of this hospital."

"Walk?"

"I promise, in fact, your physiotherapy starts today."

"And my…" My hand hovers over the large bandage still wrapped around my head.

"Time will tell." He brushes over it as if my memories, my mind, everything I have ever known is unimportant. "In the meantime, are you up to visitors?"

"I have a visitor?"

"You do. Would you like to see him?"

"Who is it?"

"Why don't we wait and see if you can work that out on your own."

I chew on my bottom lip and nod.

"Wonderful. I'll go get him."

My stomach knits itself into a hard ball. I watch the nurse write in my chart and force my mind to search through the fog. Like hands reaching out of a tomb, it comes to me. "Gloria!"

She looks up and smiles. "Yes darlin'." She's pretending I didn't just scream at her.

"Do you know who it is?"

Gloria's eyes narrow. "Wait and see, darlin'." She flashes me a wicked smile and my stomach squeezes.

"Wait! How do I look?" My hand flinches to my head and my fingers drift over the bandage covering my scalp. A strand of black hair hangs from it limply.

"Gorgeous." Her smile falters just a little and she squeezes my hand. "Ready?"

"I think so." I guess my expression shows all my uncertainty as Gloria squeezes my hand again. "I can stay with you if you like."

I nod, relieved and she lets me go, just as Doctor Jäger walks back in with a man whose tall frame casts a long shadow over the floor.

The man takes a few tentative steps into the room till he stands over my bed. Dirty blond hair falls across his brow and his weary smile shows off perfect teeth.

"Do you know this man?" Doctor Jäger gestures at the newcomer.

I study his face, wondering who he is. He bites his full lip and I can't read his face. It hovers somewhere between hope or anxiety.

"No." He flinches at my words.

"This is Tray. He is your boyfriend."

"Fiancé' actually," the man interjects, and all eyes suddenly fix on me.

My entire body gasps. It's not just an inhale but a tsunami of shock that runs through me.

"Hi baby," Tray says, and looms down over me. "These are for you." He hands me a bouquet of flowers and I look at them.

Gloria takes them from him and I hear a tap in the bathroom.

"I don't know who you are." My voice is gruff and angry and scared. I want to run, but my body is locked into the fucking bed. It feels heavy, and I'm getting tired.

The man stands there, looking uncomfortable. "You don't remember me?"

I scrutinise his handsome face again and rifle through the empty drawers of my mind. Then I shake my head.

He doesn't look disappointed, maybe relieved. It's odd. Or maybe I'm reading it all wrong.

He sits down on the edge of the mattress and I groan with the shift in the bed. He doesn't seem to notice my discomfort. Tray covers my hand with his and flashes me a beautiful smile. "My name is Tray. I'm your fiancé."

I lie there trying to work through the confusion, through my fog. I have so many questions.

Tray's eyes keep flinching to the bandage covering my forehead. "It's okay, the doctors told me you might not remember."

I focus on my breathing. At least that is one thing I know how to do.

In.

Out.

In.

Out.

"Do you want to ask me anything?"

"How…" The question falls away. I bite my lip and try to form a question that will encompass all my thoughts. I can't come up with one. "I don't remember anything." I feel like a deflated balloon all stretched out of shape.

He nods as if he understands and wraps his larger hands around mine.

"We were high school sweethearts. We started dating when we were sixteen, you were the hottest girl in school. We went to prom together, and you let me pop your cherry that night too." He tips his chin at me and winks. I feel the urge to pull my hand away. "Anyway, after high school we moved to the city. We live in an apartment, you have a photography studio, and I am starting law school in the fall."

"I'm a photographer?"

He ignores my question as if I didn't ask it. "I know I said I was your fiancé, but that wasn't exactly right." He rubs his smooth chin. "The night of your accident, we had dinner reservations, and you stopped at a bottle shop to get some wine." He rolls his eyes. "I was going to ask you that night, and I was sure you were going to say yes. I hope you don't mind, but I told your dad..."

I frown, trying to puzzle together all the pieces he has just thrown out of his box. His words are like a freight train smashing against a wall inside my head.

"My dad?"

"Senator Richard Savage, you know?"

No, I don't fucking know. "Where is he?"

"He's in Switzerland. There's a global warming conference, but he sends his love."

"His love?"

"He knows you're in good hands here with me, so he didn't feel the need to rush home, especially not during a campaign year."

Somewhere inside me, I feel a little girl snap in half. It's a familiar sensation. I push it away for now.

"Look, I know it's a lot to take in, baby, but you're here. You survived. We can just pick up where we left off. I love you so much." He leans over as if to kiss me and I flinch away, shooting pain through my entire body. I whimper like an injured animal.

Gloria is at my side a second later and Doctor Jäger clears his throat. "I think Tove's had enough introductions for one day. You are more than welcome to wait outside or here with her if she'd like. Her physio session doesn't start for another twenty minutes."

"No, I think I'll go. I have to study. Looks like my baby is in good hands." He winks at Gloria who doesn't look impressed then flashes me an odd smile. "See you tomorrow, baby."

"Tomorrow?"

But he is already out of the room.

Disappointment ripples through me. I hoped he would stay. I have questions. A myriad of black holes I need him to fill. He mentioned my father but nothing about my mum, or why no one has been here to visit me… or have I forgotten them all? I want to know about the photography thing he mentioned. The questions crash inside my head like asteroids, all desperate to reach a destination but too set on a collision course.

Gloria checks my IV.

"Are you okay?"

"I think so, I'm just so confused…"

"I know, darlin'. That will happen with your type of injury."

"Gloria?"

"Yeah?"

"Will I get my memory back?"

"You'll have to ask the doctor, honey I can't—"

"Please, just tell me the truth."

Gloria sighs, a long deep exhale, and looks me square in the eyes. "In most cases, memory comes back. It takes a few days or weeks. In more severe injuries it can take months." She busies herself with my curtain. "In very rare cases, it never comes back."

I swallow her words like a hard pill. "What if mine never does?"

"Then take it as an opportunity to start over, darlin'. We all have baggage, and maybe you have a chance to leaves yours at the door and walk away." Her eyes flick to the door that Tray just walked through. "Lunch is on its way and then your first physio session."

"Physio?"

"Yes, darlin'. Doctor Jäger just mentioned it."

"Oh, right…" I chew on my bottom lip, feeling stupid.

"Physio is a good sign, darling. It means you're strong enough to start your recovery towards healing and walking and getting out of here." She smiles at me and presses a few buttons.

"I'll see you this afternoon before I go home."

I nod. "Thanks, Gloria."

She presses her lips together in a thin smile and leaves.

⁓⋅☙

Adrian

My jaw twitches as the elevator door opens and some overgrown Ken doll bumps right into me. The asshole is way too engrossed in his phone call to notice. He makes endless promises about how his sacrifice will benefit them both once he gets all her family's money. He doesn't look up or apologise.

I let it go. I have other things to think about. Other people. People like Tove Savage. Thoughts of her have been eating me alive, anticipation gnawing at me like a hungry insect, nibbling at my patience until I could be in the same room as her again.

Air jams in my lungs and my heart constricts as I walk into her room. The swelling around her face has come down, and she looks like herself again, too much like herself. Almost. Her eyes fall on me and my heart stumbles, hoping like a fool for something that is never going to happen.

Her eyes narrow, scrutinising the long slash carved across my face. I wait for her to adjust. I wait for her to remember.

Neither happens.

"Hi, Miss Savage, my name is Adrian."

"Hi Adrian." She clears her throat like my name is lodged in her throat, "You can call me Tove."

"Okay, Tove." Tove. Tove. Tove fucking Savage. I want to scream her name in her face and watch as my voice makes her skin crawl like hers did to mine.

I edge nearer to the bed and look at her broken body, held together with tape and staples and a back brace. Like a strange Frankenstein creation. A beautiful broken monster that I have to fix.

I grab her file and read the report that I already have memorised. I know about every break and tear, every cut and fracture and minor trauma. I could trace my fingers along every bruise and abrasion, without much thought.

I shake my head, chasing away the thought like sunlight chasing away shadows and school my face. Tove is just another patient, but one with which I have a long and devastating history. A history which she can't remember and I wish I could forget.

I put the file down and step around the bed. "I am your physiotherapist, and together you and I are going to work on keeping your legs strong and strengthening your core and back muscles as they heal until you can walk out of here."

Her face changes, the cords of her neck stretch taut. I freeze.

"Tove?"

Her eyes refocus on my face, the tip of her tongue licks her bottom lip and sends a shiver down my back.

"Tove?"

"Yeah?"

"Did they talk to you about walking? About your recovery?"

Her face scrunches up in the way it always did and I bite the inside of my lip, watching her brain try and piece it all together.

"I'm pretty sure."

Her eyes fling to the ceiling and tears pool in her icy blue eyes which swim in red swollen lakes.

"You don't remember?"

She bites her lip but doesn't respond.

"Tove, you don't have to be brave with me."

Her eyes shoot to mine as if a flicker of something switched on in her brain. My heart pounds in my chest but then she turns her head away again and nods.

"Would you like me to remind you?"

⁕

Tove

Adrian's hands travel up and down my foot, using just enough pressure to make me want to scream in pain, but also in pleasure. His hands are smooth and strong against my battered body which tenses and softens at his touch.

He talks at the same time as his hands touch me and I want to listen, I do, but I feel as if I might melt away. My body screams, but it's not in pain or pleasure, it's in desperation. Somewhere inside of me I can hear a voice. I can feel it vibrate, howling against a glass pane which mutes it. Like my body remembers something imprinted on it, like a knock against my soul and yet, my brain can't translate it. My stupid broken brain can't put the framework of the puzzle together and the voice fades and disappears into a dark void inside.

Adrian keeps talking as he touches me. His voice is timber and deep like the forest of his eyes. This man looks as if he walked out of an enchanted forest where he spent all day taming wolves and chopping wood. His broad shoulders flex as he sweeps over my calve with his massive paw.

"Tove?" His voice drips through my thoughts.

"Yeah?"

"Did you hear me?"

"What?"

"How is the pressure?"

"Okay. Fine." I feel heat rise to the tips of my ears as his palms knead my calf and my body screams for more. His mouth twitches in the faintest of smiles as he moves up my leg, twisting, and my body burns with his touch. I never want it to end. His warm hands slide up to my thigh and I whimper.

He freezes. "Did I hurt you?" His face is creased.

"No." My face feels flushed and I feel trapped. Ridiculous. Held down by machines and straps and a man that should be swinging an axe somewhere, and all I can think about is what he might look like under that long-sleeved shirt of his. "It feels good."

His face visibly relaxes and he continues working. I watch him as his hands inflict the most agonising pleasure on my sore limbs. The way he sucks down on his thick bottom lip when he concentrates, and how his eyes narrow when he examines every inch of my skin, the way the long scar tears through the middle of his face and pulls and tugs as his face moves, splitting his beautiful face into two.

When he's done massaging and manipulating my muscles, he gives me exercises to do. They are not hard, or they shouldn't be, but everything hurts, and everything feels like a great big effort. By the time we are done I am exhausted and breathless, and I've been lying on my back the entire session.

I feel pathetic.

"You did an amazing job today." Adrian smiles for the first time since he walked into my room and I think my bones just turned to dust inside of me.

"It doesn't feel like it." I wipe sweat from the parts of my forehead that are not still covered in the thick bandage.

"Don't be so hard on yourself, your body suffered major trauma. It takes time to heal."

"Is that what happened to you?"

His eyes twitch over to mine. I regret the question immediately. "Sorry, sorry, I—"

"I'll see you tomorrow, Tove."

He walks out of the room and leaves me in a puddle of

sweat and regret. I feel the loss of him on my body. It's screaming at me again, but the voices are jumbled, and I can't understand what they are saying.

Before I can think much more about it, Gloria is back to change my bandages and soon the meds will kick in and my world will turn to black.

⁓

Adrian

Sweat drips from my chin and hits the floor. My gloved hands smash against the boxing bag. I've been at it for too long. My body is in pain. Not the good kind. It's straining. It needs rest. I have pushed my muscles past exertion thirty minutes ago. I'm moving by sheer willpower alone, but I can still feel her. No matter how many times I punch the bag, her skin still burns my palms, her soft whimpers invade a space inside my brain that cannot forget them.

Tove Savage has smashed her way into my life again and I want to hate her. I want to stay the broken eighteen-year-old boy she used and betrayed. But I can't, because as much as I hate to admit it, my heart hasn't beaten so fast in four years, my body hasn't felt so alive, my entire being hasn't tingled with joy for years and after just an hour with her all I want to do is hold her, have her, possess her.

I fight these feeling, beating them with my fists, but I know no matter how hard I fight, it will always be Tove fucking Savage, because no matter how hard I try to pretend, that woman has always carried the only part of me that really mattered. My heart.

I suck in air, trying to fill my burning lungs and head to the shower, peeling away my gloves and clothes, heavy with sweat. The scalding shower pelts against my skin in a final attempt to wash away all these feelings bubbling to the surface, to remove the stain of her hold on me. But even as my cock gets hard and my hand starts to move along its shaft all I can see is Tove.

⁓☙

The overgrown Ken doll is in the middle of talking her ear off, her eyes are glazed over and he doesn't even notice. Her fingers are entwined through her hair, pulling.

"He's the best plastic surgeon in town, I'm sure he can ta—"

"Morning Tove," I interrupt.

Tray flinches at my voice and sends me an irritated glance.

"Hi, Adrian." Tove's voice slices through me and makes Tray's head swivel around again. This time he takes a long hard look, his eyes narrowing as if he is trying to place me.

"Why are *you* here?" He springs from his chair and glares at me. "Are you a nurse?" His mouth flinches in a smile as he takes in my name tag.

"I'm her physio." I keep my voice steady, but my skin tingles. What the fuck is this douchebag doing here? I recognise him straight away. The man from the elevator. I take a closer look at him and step back as if I've been bitten. King Douchebag is here, with Tove, in this hospital room. Before I finish the thought, he is talking at me.

"I'm Tray, her fiancé." He sneers and his eyes gleam with menace.

"Nice to meet you," I offer, but don't move. Neither of us move, but our eyes lock as his lip curls.

"Have we met before?" he pretends. Tray is very good at pretending.

"We shared an elevator a few days back."

His face pales a few shades and he grimaces as if he's tasted something bitter.

"Yeah well, okay." He turns back to Tove, who looks at me apologetically. I'd forgotten that look, it used to be one she wore just after she started dating King Douche. "Don't worry, we will make you beautiful again. See you later, baby."

Tray bends down to kiss her and she turns her head. His kiss lands on her ear. I bite the inside of my lip. He marches out of the room, his cheeks a shade of crimson.

"Congratulations."

Tove's head turns towards me, and for the first time, I notice her bandage is gone. "For what?"

Her long black hair is set loose around her face, the strands pulled forwards, covering her left eye.

"I didn't realise you were engaged."

Her face creases. "Me neither, but I mean… thank you… I guess."

She didn't know she was engaged to the King. I inhale to keep from smirking. "Have you kept your exercises up?"

"Yes." She breaks into a smile, the pride practically slipping off her.

"So, are you ready to stand up?"

Her eyes widen, "Today? Already?"

"Today, now. We discussed it yesterday."

"I'm not sure…"

I reach the edge of the bed and look into the glacial depths. "I'll be right here with you." I can see the glacier melting and all I want to do is dive into her frozen waters.

I lower the bedrail and look to her face. "Ready?"

She gives an unsteady shake of the head and I grab her torso. I feel the muscles tense as my fingers tighten around her and I wonder if the response is to my touch or her anxiety.

I roll Tove to her side and the hair falls away from her face. The red angry gash stares back at me, the black stitches like twisted ivy. She catches my look and tries to cover up. "They're coming out tomorrow…" she mumbles.

"Keep your spine neutral, Tove, just like we spoke about."

I can see her spiralling. There are too many things at once. She is like a phone that hasn't been updated for too long, glitching and going around in circles. I lower myself so that my face is right by hers, my hand still holding her body in place.

"Breathe, Tove," I say, and suck in a deep breath. She mimics me and we breathe together, like a single being, one breath that flows through the both of us. I can feel the warmth of her breath as it blows in my face, her eyes slammed shut, her body relaxing.

"Open your eyes, Tove, look at me."

Her eyes are heated blue flames, burning bright into mine.

"I've got you. I won't let you go."

"Promise?" she whispers.

"Promise." I inhale a shuddering breath and stand up again. "Just like we talked about, neutral spine, legs off the bed, push yourself up."

She grimaces and strains against her own body, then pushes up and sits up on the bed. All her features instantly change. She squeals in glee. Actually squeals. I felt the joy as it radiates like an EMP across the room.

"I did it."

"You did." I chuckle, swept away by the wave. "Now stand." I push the walker to the edge of the bed and take a minute step back. Her eyes flicker between me and the metal frame, but they're not full of fear, they are full of determination. She grabs the frame, sucks in a deep breath and pulls herself up.

Her face is like sunshine in a cup, it's a spring day in full bloom, it's freshly cut grass and a cloudless sky.

"I'm standing!" she shrieks and my heart slams against my chest as her joy seeps beneath my skin. "Adrian, look."

I smile at her, my body clenched, tightly rooted in place

because all I want to do is go over to her and pull her into my arms and tell her she is amazing. All I want to do it kiss her till I swallow up every inch of happiness and fill myself with it.

"I could just kiss you." She blurts out and the storm in my stomach intensifies. "I can't believe I'm doing this." She continues as if she hadn't just stabbed me in the heart.

I clear my throat and step closer. "Would you like to try walking?"

She looks at me, her eyes wide, her smile stretching. "You think I could?"

"A few steps today and then we have to start working on your scar tissue."

The smile falls from her face and her hand reaches to her forehead, as her eyes travel the length of my scar.

"It's not that bad."

"Is that what they told you too?" Her voice is humourless, and she looks down, veiling her face with her hair.

"Have you seen it yet?"

"No." She bites her lip and shakes her head.

"If you take ten steps, I'll bring you a mirror."

"You will?"

"Ten steps."

"Ten?"

I nod.

She braces herself against the walker, her knuckles whitening with the tightening grip. She steps, the joy is back, and it's endless as if a dam of happiness has burst inside of her.

She counts them out loud, motivating herself. I feel like a passenger coming along for her journey.

On step six, she falters.

"Just four more steps, Tove."

"I can't. I'm too tired."

"And you'll be tired again tomorrow and the next day, but you have to take four more steps for me, Tove."

"I can't."

"You can and you will, because I know how much you want that mirror."

She shoots me a look that I can't quite read and then puts another foot forward. Her steps are minute. They shouldn't really count, but I can see how hard she is working. I can see how her legs begin to shake as she holds herself up. She grimaces each time she inches forward, and her face floods with elation with each tiny gain. My heart churns and I fight the urge to hold her and tell her she'll be okay.

"Three."

"Two."

"One."

She counts out and her face turns to mine. Sweat peppers her brow and her breaths are quick and shallow as though she's just run a marathon. Her face, a mask of exhaustion and elation. Breathtaking.

"Well done, Tove." I memorise her face, forcing my lungs to work.

I help her back into the bed and she sucks in a deep breath.

"My reward?"

"Right."

I go to the bathroom and grab a mirror. Then I come to stand by the side of her bed. "Are you ready?"

She nods and holds out her hand.

I know this feeling, the desire to see, the fear of what awaits.

"Are you sure?"

"Just give it to me."

I place the mirror in her hand. Tove gasps as she studies her face, her fingers hovering over the deep gash and stitches that decorate half her scalp.

"I'm hideous."

"You're beautiful, Tove."

She doesn't answer. Like she didn't hear a single thing I said.

I wait.

Silence.

She needs to process. The thing that you stare at every day, forever changed in a way you have no control over, marred, scarred, deformed. You can't hide it from the rest of the world, they all know you are marked. It's like death. There's grieving for your former life, a life where people didn't judge you by that one scar, that one mark that is so visible and angry, that lets everyone make assumptions, make judgements, make decisions they didn't know they were going to make.

She lets the mirror drop from her hand, her eyes glazed over, staring at the ceiling.

"Tove?"

She flinches at her name as if she's only just remembered I'm there.

"You need to roll over. I need to work on your back today."

Once she's on her stomach, I unbuckle the brace and open her hospital gown. The long, jagged scar along her spine is like an angry sea, with bands of skin all crashing into one another in an angry wave.

Her back is creamy and long and the swells of her ass peek from the towel.

"You must think I'm so vain."

I scoff. She's always been vain, it's why she picked an accessory she can take with her in public and not a freak like me. "It's human nature. We chase perfection."

"How do you…"

"Live with it?"

She nods.

I shrug and drop some oil onto my hands, rubbing them together, my fingers itching to be on her skin, to feel her.

My hands fall on her back and she tenses for a second. Her flesh is soft beneath my palms as I glide up and down the length of her back.

"It takes time." I increase pressure as I manoeuvre my hands along her spine, breaking apart scar tissue. She moans and my body reacts in all the wrong ways. All the right ways.

"How much time?" It's somewhere between a moan and a cry and my body aches for her. I swallow hard and let my hands do what they do best. Heal.

I shrug as my palms trace the worn muscles of her back. "Some days you feel like you've accepted it. You let the looks and the remarks and the whispers just float by you like clouds. Other days they weigh heavily on you and even when you try to shake it off and remind yourself that you are more than just that fucking thing on your face, it still hurts. The scar we carry is on the outside but it's only a doorway to more scarring on the inside. You just have to brace yourself, love yourself and find someone who sees beyond your skin."

She shudders, and I wonder if it's my words or my touch that make her body quiver. My fingers itch to explore more of her, to plunge down beyond the towel and…

"Do you have someone like that?"

My heart stumbles at the question. "I did."

"And now?"

"And now we are done." I wrench my hands away from her skin and close her robe, buckling the back brace. "How do you feel?"

"I don't know."

I help her roll to her back and her eyes hold mine for a moment.

I nod. "Give it time, Tove,"

"Why? Does time heal everything?"

"No. But it helps." I break away from the bed and wa[lk] towards the door. "See you tomorrow, Tove."

I catch my breath, forcing air in and out of my lungs. My legs burn with effort and my body is covered in a sheen of sweat. Even after my run I haven't sweated Tove out of my system. I can feel her everywhere. She is my affliction, spreading throughout my body like poison. I can't find the antidote, and, after touching her, I'm not sure I want to. The feel of her soft skin under my fingertips stirs up dangerous memories, memories my body aches for and my mind struggles to forget.

I want to keep hating her, I try to shake her off, but she is like sunburn. A red angry sting on my skin. Revenge was meant to taste better, feel better.

I pull myself together, reminding myself that I am her doctor, reminding myself she is engaged to King Douche, reminding myself that our shot is finished. That it never even began. That I shouldn't be doing this. Any of this.

I think of the long ugly wound across her forehead, the big staples holding the contents of her head inside. She'll need to be guided through. And King Douche won't be the guy to do it.

I suck in a long breath and think about helping Tove, helping myself. Helping myself get over Tove. I try to force myself to concentrate on that ugly mark, knowing it will forever carve her forehead, stain the perfect skin, mar the perfect complexion and structure. But all I can think of is how beautiful she looks, all broken and vulnerable and fucking human.

Like me.

Tove

I've been looking at the clock for far too long. Tray is here again talking at me. He doesn't come every day which I find to be a relief. I feel underwater when he is with me. I can't be heard in his vortex. His current sucks me in but suffocates me. I have a niggling feeling that he is hiding something. He skirts around the things he should be saying.

He's been telling me about our relationships, holidays we've been on, and people we hang around with, parties we've attended. But he never shows me pictures and his face grows dark every time I ask. And he still hasn't brought me my damn phone.

His gorgeous smile catches me, and I smile back, nodding. I tune back in. "- and don't worry, I'm sure your dad will pay for the best surgeon in town to get that off your face." His eyes flick over to my forehead and his smile falls into a grimace.

I grab my hair and pull it over my face. He keeps bringing it up. I chew my lower lip and glance at the clock. My heart ticks over with the seconds,

Three,

Two,

One.

"Good afternoon, Tove, Tray." His voice smothers me and I catch my breath.

"Adrian." His eyes flicker to the hair across my forehead and darkness clouds his eyes.

"How do you feel after yesterday's session?"

"Excited."

"Yesterday?" Tray stands up, his brow creased. "What happened yesterday?" His shoulders square and he faces Adrian as if he is about to launch a missile strike.

"Tove took her first steps, didn't she tell you?" Adrian's head cocks and his gaze flickers from me to Tray.

Tray turns to me, his eyes wide. "You walked?" His voice is strained, unhappy, tense.

My mouth feels dry and I nod, unable to talk.

"What about your memory? Is that coming back too? What did the doctor say?"

"They don't know when that will happen, it can take a week or a month or longer…"

Tray turns to Adrian and raises both eyebrows, expecting something more.

Adrian moves closer to the bed and puts the rail down. He looks at me as he speaks, "The brain and the back are not connected in that way. The brain remembers how to make the body work, but memories are stored elsewhere. When they are ready to surface, they will."

"What does that mean?" Tray shifts his weight. He sounds agitated.

"Would you like to watch Tove walk today?"

"Maybe later, I have to go." He seems flustered. "See you later, baby."

"Tray?" I call back after him, "can you please bring my phone with you next time you come?"

"Sure, sure," he mutters, then runs out of the room.

Adrian searches my face.

"He's just busy…" I bite my lip. Is he? Why am I defending him? Is this how we always were?

"That's none of my business. Only you are my business, Tove." The way he says the second part of that sentence sends a shiver down my broken spine, like a slithering promise.

I sit up and pull myself onto the walking frame.

"Today you will walk to the door. Then back to bed."

I take my first step and feel shards in my feet, like stepping on a thousand tiny knives. Adrian's smooth timber voice coaxes me forward with each step. He's like a balm to my searing pain. All I want is to be near to him. Near enough to smell him, the intoxicating mix of pine and earth as if he just walked out of a forest.

By the time I am halfway to my bed, my heart is pounding, and air feels like a luxury only healthy people get to enjoy. The pain in my hip and back stabs deeply and I want to scream, I want to break, I want to snap it in half to make it all go away.

"Ten more steps, Tove." His luxurious voice cuts through my agony, like ice on hot skin. It leaves a cool trail.

"I don't know if I can."

"Of course, you can."

"No." I whimper.

He edges close to me, his broad shoulders looming over me, his breath hot on my neck. "Take ten more steps for me Tove and I will give you ten more minutes of my time today. I will make that pain melt away."

I swallow hard. The thought of his hands on me for an extra ten minutes feels like fuel for days. I suddenly have the motivation to cross a desert, run a marathon and climb Mount Everest, just to have him touch me again.

My body recognises him in a way that is primal and needy. He stirs things in me that a doctor should not be stirring in his patient. I don't care. While I have him all to myself, I will enjoy the sensation of being touched, because I have a feeling that once I am out in the world, things will be very different for me. I may not remember my past, but I have a pretty vivid image of my future.

I push through the pain and arrive, exhausted, at the bed. Adrian has a strange expression, one I wished I could read, one distorted by the long ravine slicing his otherwise beautiful face.

Once I am on my stomach, Adrian's hands begin their long, leisurely torture of my muscles and scar tissue. It is exquisite pain and one my body aches for.

"Adrian? Can I ask you something?"

"Okay."

"Do we –"

"Tove!" An older man bursts into the room, followed by two others.

I jerk at the sound of my name, my body feeling the aftershocks. I moan at the pain travelling down my spine.

The man examines me, his eyes set on my back where Adrian still works, undeterred, as if nothing has happened. "Sorry I took so long to get here… work… you know how it is…"

I look at the man. He's dressed in a tailored suit that matches his jet-black hair tigered with grey stripes and slicked to the side. His dark blue eyes stormy as his gaze flickers from my forehead to my back.

"Who are you?" I finally ask and he looks taken aback, as if I have stabbed him.

"You don't recognise your own father?"

Tears well in my eyes as I shake my head. "You're my dad?"

The man turns to Adrian, flinches at the sight of him, and corrects himself. "I thought she'd be better by now."

Adrian's jaw twitches and his hands come to rest on my lower back. Heat radiates from them into my core, a comforting sensation, as if he is giving me his strength.

"She is getting much better every day. Ask her."

"Can we have some privacy, please?"

"Visiting hours are between two and four. Right now, Tove is having her physio session with me. Each session is integral to her recovery and can't be missed. You can stay if you like, but your men need to leave, please."

Adrian resumes his massage as if there's no one in the room but us, his strong hands manipulating my muscles. I clutch the pillow, holding in the moans building inside me. I want to squirm, I want to clench my legs, I want to jump up and wrap myself around him.

The man — my father — I correct myself, trying to wrap my head around the concept, clears his throat.

"Tove? Can you tell him we need to talk alone?"

"You should come back later. I need my sessions to heal." I bury my head into the pillow and resist the urge to bite through the fabric.

"Tove?"

Our eyes lock. We're at an impasse. It feels familiar somehow.

My father turns to his men and nudges toward the door. They step outside and leave the three of us in a strange silence.

He grabs a chair and pulls it to the side of my bed, then sits and takes my hand in his. I waver, wondering if I should snatch it away, but I feel Adrian's reassuring pressure on my back, a nuance of a touch like he is telling me it's okay. I listen.

"Hi sweetheart, I'm so sorry darling." The man's stormy eyes pool with tears and he examines my face, while his creases, the furrows of his forehead deepening. "I should have come sooner but I was told it wasn't *that* bad."

"By who?"

"Your fiancé." The way he says it makes me think of acid, as though he needs to spit it out of him.

"You don't approve?"

"As long as you're happy."

I shrug. The idea of happiness is laughable. "Why did it take you so long to come?"

"I had to work."

"*Had* to?"

He rakes a hand through his hair and let's go of my hand, sinking back into his chair. "Not now, Tove."

I suck on my lower lip, wondering how many times we've had this fight before.

"Can you remember anything at all?"

"No." I can feel that pressure again as if Adrian knows everything I am going to feel before I do. His fingers dig into me, holding in me in one piece. "Can you help me remember?"

"How?"

"The doctors say it's good for me to hear about before. They say it might help trigger memories."

His gaze keeps flickering from my scar to the clock on the wall and his whole body looks like it's been packed with dynamite and ready to explode.

"I didn't have much time, Tovey. It's an election year. I thought...." He sighs, rubbing his hands on his thighs, a gold Rolex slips and down his wrist. "I didn't realise..." He gestures to my whole body - as if that means anything.

"Tell me about my mum?"

The pressure of Adrian's hands is deep again, like he is trying to reach my soul with his touch. My dad's eyes widen and flicker, his mouth stretches into a long thin line.

"Tovey... I'm not sure it's a good idea."

"Please."

His dark eyes meet mine and I can see the sadness that lies at the bottom of his ocean, it's anchored into his depths, and I feel a flicker of regret.

"She's unwell, it's why she isn't here."

I feel Adrian's hands sink into me, holding me, telling me to prepare. I suck in a long breath and wait for this stranger to keep talking.

"It was early onset dementia, there was no explanation. One day she was fine, and the next, she just started forgetting things. Our anniversary, the milk, where she put the car keys. Later it got worse, repeating herself all the time, and she'd get lost..." His face is drawn and ashen, while Adrian keeps me from falling apart. "I had to travel for work, so I put her in care."

"You abandoned her?"

"No."

"You just left her?" My voice rises in pitch. Something dislodges in my chest like a savage desperation to protect my creator, one I can't remember but somehow tugs at my heart.

"It's not like that, Tove, I told you."

"Tell me again, 'cause I can't fucking remember anything!" I scream at him and his face falls while Adrian tries to soothe me wordlessly.

The man takes my had but this time I snatch it away. He looks at me and scrubs a hand over his face. "I guess I deserve that."

His composure falls away a little more and he leans in, so that our eyes meet, and for the first time he looks at me. Really looks at me as though he can see me, beyond the broken face and fractured body.

"I *had* to put her in care. Seeing my best friend vanish before my eyes was the most difficult thing I've ever had to endure. She became a stranger."

"A liability."

"No! Your mother was, *is*, everything to me. As are you."

I scoff, "You have a funny way of showing it." I hiss as Adrian kneads my burning flesh.

"Tove, I need you to understand. I couldn't just stand by and watch her be a helpless useless thing. She didn't even know who she was, who we were." His eyes are full of fear. He is afraid that I won't remember him again, that he has lost everything. I find it difficult to find any compassion for him.

I give a humourless laugh, the sound hollow and angry. "You abandoned us both."

He shakes his head again. Yanking his phone from his pocket, he unlocks it and shows me the screen picture.

A stunning woman that looks like half of me stands with the man who sits by my bed. The girl in the middle is a younger version of me, one before the accident, with flawless skin and a happy smile, maybe fourteen. Maybe younger.

He gazes at the picture for a long time, his fingers tracing the cold frozen glass. "This picture was the last one of the three of us together. It was a beautiful day and your mum wanted ice cream on the beach, so we drove around for three hours. Not because the beach is far, but because your mother kept changing her mind and getting lost and frustrated. I indulged her, but I think it was because I already knew it would be the last time we were all together." He sighs and his large frame seems to shrink in the seat.

"We had our ice cream and took the picture by the pier." His voice falls away. Cracking.

"What then?"

"Tove… not this memory…" he begs, but I have no mercy for this pathetic man who so easily lets the people in his life be put away in boxes to be cared for by strangers. Who forsakes the ones he loves, who deserted her…me.

"Tell me!" Adrian's hands are there and I feel the urgency in them, as if they are unsure themselves if they can keep me from falling to pieces.

My dad's eyes glaze over and he is lost somewhere in a past I used to know. "She had to go to the toilet. We waited, and waited, and after a while I sent you to go get her, but she was gone." His mouth twists as if his heart has just been pierced by an icy shard. "By the time we found her, she was dehydrated and disoriented, walking on the side of the highway. She'd had her worst episode yet and it scared her, all of us."

He gives me a sad smile. "That night she asked me to put her away. I refused, I promised I'd look after her. But she *begged* me. We both cried that night. I resisted her as much as I could, but in the end, she was always the stronger one of the two of us. She refused to let me end my dreams and stay at home looking after a shadow. She didn't want us- you - to remember her like that. She wanted you to know how much she loved you." He clears his throat as if it's clogged by all his emotions. "Your mother loves you very much. She didn't want to cause us worry or pain. She knew that in a home she would be looked after, medicated, safe, and we could always visit."

"Did we?" I search for my voice.

My heart wrenches at the sight of his face and I don't think I want him to answer any more. "You didn't believe me that she asked to go, and you cut us both out. You were only thirteen and angry and sad but neither of us could get through to you."

I absorb his words and we sit in silence as I let the pain settle in around me. "Have I seen her...since?"

"Yes, we had a neighbour boy who was your friend." He shoots a look at Adrian. "I think he talked you into going, and you did, once a month for the last few years, until it became too hard."

I swallow a lump that's formed in my throat.

"The last time she had a day of clarity she called me, but I was in a meeting and she left me this message." He plays with his phone, then holds it up. A beautiful rich feminine voice reaches out from the phone:

"Hi Rich. Fuck, I miss you so much, I love you, I know this is hard for you to hear but we did the right thing. Tove has been coming. I told you she'll come around. She's an amazing young girl, you're doing a great job with her, she will grow up to be an incredible human." The voice breaks a little as she goes on, "I miss you every day, the two of you, but I want you both to move on. This life, it's so fleeting, so short. Find your happiness and grab onto it with both hands because it can be snatched away at any second." She clears her throat, but the quiver is still there. "Find it in your heart to forgive yourself, darling, thank you for loving me fiercely enough to let me go. I hope our baby girl finds a love like ours that burns so deeply, you will always be my one and only. Forgive me for leaving you so young, for leaving our daughter, I would do –"

The recording ends abruptly and a silence so heavy falls on the room I am afraid to breathe, it's like we're in mourning. My dad's hand drops away and he breaks the spell. I suck in a deep breath and feel the tears rolling down my face, soaking into the pillow. Adrian's hands rest on my lower back. He doesn't move, his touch like a strong hug, reassuring and protecting me from my fracturing soul.

"I…I should go." My dad stands up and shrugs off the emotion on his face.

"Will you be back?" I say through a strangled choke and he winces as if I'd hit him.

"Of course, I'll move some things around. I'm sorry sweetheart, I really didn't know…" His shoulders drop and he stares at me for a minute unsure of what he should be doing. Then he bends awkwardly and kisses me on my brow.

"I love you, Tove." The words are spears to my heart.

He walks to the door and steps out. His two guards fall into steps behind him as he disappears.

As soon as my father has gone, I feel the sobs coming as they claw their way up my throat. It's like a rising tide that washes over me. My throat closes and I let out a barking choked sound. I am held under water, breathless and gagging.

A timber voice pulls me from the water like a drifting log on the surface of the raging storm inside of me.

"Tove?" he calls me. I open my eyes to find his face inches from mine. His long fingers brush away the hair from my face and tuck it behind my ear. His touch sends a ripple along my body.

"I'm so confused. I don't know how I am supposed to feel about anything." I suck in a frayed breath, my head sinking into my pillow. I feel helpless. I try to push myself up so that I can turn onto my back and pain shoots up my body. I whimper and fall back down like a wounded animal. I feel crushed. "I feel *so alone.*"

Adrian looks at the clock and something passes across his face. He is at the door in two steps. I want to cry out to him, to reach for him, beg him to stay, but then he closes it and I hear the distinct click of a lock. He returns to the bed and kneels until his face is inches from mine.

"I've got you, Tove." There is something carnal in his voice and my body tightens.

"Promise?" I whisper.

His hands are on me again and Adrian tentatively turns me to my side, then slips into the bed beside me. The mattress shifts with his weight, and he releases me, allowing my body to fall along his.

My breath hitches as his arms close around me and he draws me closer. I am enveloped in pine and earth and masculinity. The warmth of his body radiates into me, as I sink into him, soaking his T-shirt with my tears.

He lies there in his stoic silence but even as the tears rip from me, I hear the thundering of his heart, a maddening beat. He pulls me closer and I feel the hard muscles of his body, he is a rock and I am breaking against it. Against *him.* And he lets me.

I can breathe again as I hold onto him. I open my eyes to find his. They are alive in a way I've never noticed before, the forest inside them teeming. In this moment, I can feel all of him. He is the forest and I want to lie beneath his canopy and indulge in his sunshine and feel his breeze on my face. My fingers trace the curve of his jaw then weave through his wild locks, gripping the strands, I pull him down towards me and graze his lips with mine.

His eyes grow wide, but he doesn't pull away. We are frozen like fallen trees on a forest floor. Everything is silent, my heart, the storm, the world, it waits for us. His grip slides over my waist, loose and unsure, then a second later, tighter, resigned. His fingers dig into me as his mouth closes over mine.

The first kiss is slow, almost hesitant. His soft lips are warm, setting my nerve endings on fire, igniting my skin. He gathers me against him, and kisses me harder, a soft groan, low in his throat, rumbles from somewhere inside of him, like thunder.

I move my lips against his and they answer with urgent intensity. His tongue slips inside my mouth and I moan into him, and he shudders against the sound. He grips me with violent desperation, and I latch onto him with twisted hungry need. I want to melt into him like a glacier in summer. My body screams for him, an ache so familiar like it knows him, like we should be one.

"Tove." He breaks away, suddenly stiff. "Tove, stop. Shit, I can't do this." He stumbles backwards and almost falls from the bed, then slips me onto my back.

"I'm sorry, I'll see you tomorrow."

Without another word or explanation, he bolts from the room as though he has been stung, and my tattered heart sinks, and I want to break all over again.

⁓⋅❦

Adrian

F uck fuck fuck fuck fuck.

I am hiding in the staff lounge, my hands tearing through my hair, the taste of salty tears on my lips. She fucking kissed me, she fucking kissed me and I kissed her back because all I wanted was her, and then I ran away like a fucking coward. I'm not going to lose everything I have built here over Tove. That's not part of the plan.

I need to get away from her, but it's already too late. I know it. I'm already addicted to the feel of her, to the look of hunger in her eyes every time she sees me, to the way her body calls to mine. I'm an addict, and tomorrow I will need another hit or my skin will want to tear itself from my body and the old pain will rise to the surface. The hate, the scorn, the anguish.

Fuck.

I slam my locker shut and call HR, citing an onset of a migraine, asking for the rest of the day off. In the two years I've worked here I've never taken a day off, haven't asked for a holiday, came in early, left late… it's a perk when you have no one waiting for you at home. The HR woman signs me out and wishes me good health.

I get in my car, slamming the door behind me. I clutch the wheel and grit my teeth.

Fuck.

Something moves in my periphery and I turn my head. I see the couple. They are kissing in the front seat, but it seems more than a kiss, as if they are praying mantises, each trying to devour the other. It's brutal and angry and possessive. A spark of jealousy ignites inside me, it trickles, licking my hungry aching flesh. I can't wrench my eyes away, their passion taunts me, lashing out with sharp teeth. When the woman comes up for air, I see the man. King Douche in all his glory. His head falls back against the headrest and his eyes slam shut, while the woman's hand works just below the steering wheel. Acid curdles in my stomach.

I rev my engine and my tyres screech as I pull off. His eyes lock onto mine and he pushes the woman away from him, his face flushed and flustered.

I grab the steering wheel, my grip threatening to snap the wheel in half. Tove is a big girl, she can make her own mistakes. I know I am lying to myself as I tear down the road. I drive aimlessly. The city disappears behind me, the cars vanish until, without meaning to, I drive down a familiar track lined with evergreen trees. Mr Cunningham's decrepit house is on the verge of collapse, rotting away, like him. I heard he was dead for at least a week before they found him. Stink like that is hard to wash away.

Dad's pick up is in the driveway, and so is the new red Toyota he's bought for Kate. I kill the engine and sit watching the house. I dig my hands into my scalp, then climb out of the car. I don't want to be here. Too many memories stain these walls.

I take a galvanising breath and knock on the door. It swings open and Kate freezes mid-motion, mid-sentence. She stands, clinging to the door, just staring at me. My presence has somehow cast a spell on her that I don't know how to break. I wait for her to thaw but she seems stuck, unable to move.

Dad walks into the lounge. "Hey Kate, who is…" His mouth drops open when he sees me, and he rushes to the door. His voice breaks the uncomfortable spell and Kate moves out of the way as he slings himself onto me and wraps his arms around me. "Adrian." The disbelief is thick and ugly.

He breaks away and a look of concern passes across his face. "What a great surprise." He moves into the house and waits for me to follow before slamming the door shut. Maybe he thinks I might change my mind and run away. Maybe he thinks caging me is the only way to keep me around. Or safe.

"Hi Kate." I nod to the petite blonde who watches me with large brown eyes. I don't mind her. She's made Dad happy again and he deserves that. She's made him come alive again, and I like that about her. She makes him smile in a way I never could, plus she makes him wash, and get out of the house and live.

"Hi Adrian." Her face breaks into a sad smile. "Can I offer you something to drink? We were just about to have a coffee."

"Did I interrupt? I can come back another time…"

"No!" My dad steps in front of the door. "You're not interrupting anything. Come in. Please."

I look to Kate, who nods.

"A coffee would be great. Thank you."

"Great." She smiles and walks off to the kitchen.

"It's so good to see you son, you look so…"

"Different?" I scoff.

"Big."

"I've joined a boxing gym, have a great coach."

"Boxing?"

"Figured my face can't get much more messed up, can it." I try to make it into a joke but his face falls. Too soon? Maybe for him it will always be too soon. I did a 360. "You seem happy."

"I am."

"I'm happy for you."

Tentatively he walks towards the couch and sits, his eyes glued to me. I follow him deeper into the room and fall into the recliner. He seems to relax a little.

He clears his throat, his movements hesitant. "Are you in some kind of trouble?"

He blurts it out and I know it's hard for him. Not because he wouldn't help, but he hates thinking that I have an ulterior motive for being there. Why else would I show up at his door unannounced after four years and ask for coffee.

"No." I can feel the question at the tip of his tongue. "Look, everything is fine, okay? I just have a patient at the hospital that's suffered some real trauma. I needed to get away and kind of ended up here."

The strain from my dad's face shifts into something else, surprise? Elation? His son felt down and he chose him as a haven.

I can't disillusion him. I just needed to clear my head, nothing more.

Kate walks in with the coffee and the three of us sit in

awkward silence and drink. It's as if they don't know how to behave around me. I can see her fingers wanting to reach out to him, instead, she shifts and slides away, deepening the space between them.

Why is that everywhere I go silence and emptiness follow?

We finish and Kate takes the cups to the kitchen. They clink in the hollow silence.

"I might head back…"

"Why? Stay for dinner. You can sleep here tonight. Drive back up in the morning." He rubs the back of his neck, and I can almost taste the desperation on his breath.

The thought of sleeping in this house again makes my stomach crawl. "Okay."

"Kate, we have a plus one for dinner." He beams at me.

Kate saunters out of the kitchen. "That's wonderful. Now that you have a young man here to help you, can you please go sort out my garage." She catches herself and seems almost apologetic. When did *our* become *hers*? I don't hold it against her. This is more her house than mine now. I hate how they both walk on eggshells around me.

"Sure thing, just tell me what you need doing." I take her out of her misery.

"This old lug can tell you. I've been nagging him for months to move stuff around so he can make more room in there for a studio."

He grabs her by the shoulders. "Who are you calling an old lug?"

I can see she wants to retort, I can see the mischief in her eyes, but as they flicker over to me the flame extinguishes. "Just go." She shakes free and heads upstairs. My dad follows her with an apologetic expression, then turns and leads the way to the garage.

My muscles burn and I wipe sweat on my sleeve as we lean against the wall. All the old furniture and unused trash now moved from one side of the space to another. Mum's old vanity is still there, boxes of things she couldn't take to the grave with her.

"Why do you keep all this stuff?"

"I don't know." His gaze drifts over the pile. "I guess at first I didn't know how to let go and then later…"

"Later?"

He sucks in a long breath and the old weariness is back on his face. "We never talked, not about what happened to her, to you…" He gestures his hands helplessly. "I guess I never knew if you dealt with it, let go of her. I kept them in case you needed them as an anchor to before."

My heartbeat feels erratic and a lump forms in my throat, clogging it, but he's right, we never did talk about it. Any of it. "I thought you needed space."

"I did, but you were a kid and then you…"

"I fell, Dad."

He nods. The silence wants to veil us again, to shield us from pain, from confrontation, from the truth. I push through it.

"Was it me?" I look to my feet as I ask *that* question.

"What?"

"Did she kill herself because of me? Is that why you couldn't look at me all those years?"

His mouth falls open and his eyes well with tears. "Is that what you've been thinking all this time? All these years?"

"Did she?" I grate through gritted teeth.

"No, Adrian! No. It was never you. She was sick. They found a tumour…"

"And she gave up on us? She didn't want to fight?" Disgust rolls through me.

Tears roll down his face and he shakes his head violently.

"No, son, she wanted to fight, she wanted to stay, she loved you so fucking much."

The words become thicker and harder as he wrenches them from his silent pit, like clay bricks lodged inside of him. "The tumour pressed against her limbic system, it grew too big too quickly and it affected everything. She lost control of everything. She didn't know what she was doing that night… she wanted to fly…"

"You never told me," I stutter, the pain gushing through me like hundreds of needles inside my bloodstream. They prick my skin all at once and I want to scream.

"You were too young, and every time I tried… and then you…" Sobs are ripping from him and he suddenly seems so small.

I feel like I have just been punched in the gut, everything I thought and believed about the way Mum took her own life was wrong. I thought she made a choice, but she never really had one. I thought she chose death over me, but she chose life. She wanted to fly, to soar, to live.

"I'm so sorry, Adrian, I should have found a way to tell you. I should have forced us to talk. I should have been a better father to you."

"You lost your wife."

"No. I lost my soulmate, the love of my life, but you…" he stammers. "You lost a mother, and, I guess, a father. I'm sorry, son."

And then he doesn't wait for permission, as if his confession has erased all the lines and walls between us. He lunges at me and wraps his hands around me. He pulls me in, cradling me in his large strong arms, and I feel safe enough to break. And I do. We cry into one another, as if we've both sprung a leak that can't be contained. Years of anguish and sadness, of hard gnawing silences, tear from us, patching us up with snot and tears and warmth, and for the first time in almost a decade I feel like I have my father back.

We pull apart and pull ourselves together, but we are different now. The ravine between us is full to the brim with water and there are ways to cross it. It's still going to be hard to sink or swim against an unfamiliar current, but at least now we have a path.

"There's something else I've been meaning to talk to you about…" Dad shifts his weight and grips the back of his neck.

"Yeah?" I scrub my hand over my jaw, skimming the thick stubble.

"I want to ask Kate to marry me." He shrinks for a second and I can see the tension creep back into his face. This new truce between us is still too fragile.

"I think that's great, Dad."

"You do?" He blooms before my eyes, growing tall.

"Sure. She makes you happy, she gives you shit, she makes you call me every week so we can breathe into the phone at one another…" At that his lips flinch with a half smile. "You need her and she clearly likes you so… please don't let me be the thing that stands in the way of your happiness."

"Son…"

"No, I know." I stop him because I know if he starts talking again, he will say all the things I don't want to hear. My nerves are already frayed and my emotions raw. I don't want more, not today. "Another day."

I guess he feels the same because he nods and pulls his jeans up, but they slip right back down.

"So, this patient of yours, giving you a hard time?"

"You can say that."

"Want to talk about it?"

I consider it. "It's Tove."

"Tove? Savage? Your Tove?" His face lights up.

"She was never my Tove." My voice is harsher than I intend, and his expression darkens.

"Wasn't she?"

I feel the heat rise inside my body, it leaks everywhere like a spilt inkwell.

"You guys used to be close."

"That was years ago."

He considers my words. "Some connections surpass time."

"Dad."

"Look Adrian, I know we've never been close, and I know *this* is new and strange. I feel it too, but son, I am not blind." He sticks his hands in his pockets like he doesn't know what else to do with them. "The way you looked at that girl, is the same way you look even saying her name."

I grind my teeth, not wanting to be here.

"Just don't wait too long, don't lose her again."

"Dad."

"I see the pain in your eyes, your heart is still bleeding for her." His hand lands on my shoulder "It won't heal, not till you go after her."

"Dad." There is a warning in my voice that he ignores completely as he continues.

"No! life is fleeting, it's short and painful most of the time and if you find just one thing, one person that brings you something other than pain, then grab it and hold onto it as tight as you can."

"It's too late."

"It's not too late! As long as you're both breathing it's not too late."

"She doesn't—" I wrench a hand through my hair. "She doesn't feel that way about me..." My emotions turn jagged as I think about the kiss, the feel of her lips, the softness of her body against mine.

"I think we both know that's bullshit." His words take me by surprise and his eyes hold mine. "Do you want her?"

I stare him down.

"Do you love her?"

His eyes bore into mine as I stand there, stoic, pretending we both don't know the answer to that.

"Then fight for her, son, because love like that, the one that burns through your veins and sets your heart alight, that's like a rare flower. Don't let her go."

My body aches and knits together. "She's engaged to someone else."

Before he can say anything more my stomach rumbles.

He looks down at his feet as he leads us out. "Let's get inside. I'm sure Kate will feed us."

⚘

Dinner is uneventful. Pleasant even. I don't recognise my own father. He smiles and cracks jokes and the way he looks at Kate make his eyes crinkle as if the very sight of her makes them happy, as if each of his body parts enjoys her differently. I try not to dwell too much on the thought. I wonder if that's how he used to be. I wish I remembered a different version of him, this version. If Mum was his soulmate and Kate a replacement, I can't begin to imagine how he would have been with her. The thoughts make me simultaneously happy and sad.

Dad walks me to my room as if he doesn't believe I'll stay if he doesn't get me across the threshold. I wish him a good night and close the door behind him. I can feel him, as he stands there behind the door. Breathing. It all feels too familiar.

I scan the room. It hadn't been touched in years. It's like a shrine, to me. A cold shiver creeps up my spine. All my old band posters hang on the walls. They are beaten up and sun burned and the Blu tack is pulling away from the walls and staining the paint with oily dots.

The desk looks just as I left it when I walked out. Cluttered with pens and books, and scarred with scratch marks. I stare at the drawers and rub my hands together. My gaze flickers to my window. To *her* window. I reach for the bottom drawer and yank it open, it falls from the rails with a thud.

I stare at the pile of papers shoved inside in a messy heap. I pull out the papers one at a time and read our one-sided conversations, the jagged writing and angry words of an obsessed, love-struck boy. The memories slice my heart with a thousand tiny paper-cuts.

I grimace at the pile now strewn across the floor in a flurry. I'm no longer that boy, but a full-grown man, angry and broken and possessed by the need for her. I will not compete for her affection, King Douche is no longer real competition. No one is. Tove is mine. She's always been mine, she's just never admitted it to herself.

All I have to do it remind her how much she needs me, wants me, loves me, and then I will rip her heart apart and leave it to bleed.

Tove

I look at the clock, knowing he is about to walk in. My entire body is burning, with shame, desire, want, need, Adrian.

"Good morning." His gravelly voice scratches under my skin.

"Hi." Heat rises to my face and I can't look at him although all I want is to see him. I feel his eyes on me.

"Can you sit up for me, Tove?"

I do, and he brings the walking frame to my bed. "Can you walk over to me?"

For the first time since he's walked in, I look at him. He is standing by a wheelchair.

My gaze lands on the chair then flickers to Adrian's eyes. The brooding darkness is back inside of them. "Are we going somewhere?"

"Yes, I have a special session planned for you today."

"What is it?"

"Take your steps and come to me. Then I'll take you."

"But you're all the way over there," I huff.

He doesn't answer. Adrian leans against the door frame waiting for me, about to take me somewhere. My entire core feels giddy. I take my first step, then another. I can feel the strength returning to my legs, I walk to Adrian and I am breathing almost normally when my walking frame jams against the door.

He smiles at me. "Well done, now sit down."

He makes no move to help or touch me at all. My heart pinches at the thought, but I adjust my back and sit down. The chair feels stiff as if it's designed to withhold my weight and keep me upright. I feel like I'm sitting in a church pew. A sheen of guilty sweat erupts along my hairline.

"Are you ready?" His voice curls around me, and I shiver.

"Where are we going?"

He ignores me and wheels me into the corridor. It's bright, and busy, lined with chairs, some occupied. The walls are decorated with floral pieces against neutral tones. He wheels me past the nurses' station where a gathering of staff centres around computers and charts. It smells different out here, sterile, numb. I miss my room already.

We wait for the elevator and he pushes me inside. The elevator starts to move, and we are alone again, and I want to scream, the silence gnawing at me.

I rub my hands on my thighs. "About yesterday…" I start but the elevator doors fly open, and three new occupants join us in the cramped space. I shut my mouth.

When the door opens again, he wheels me down a long silent corridor and we reach a large double door. He pushes it open and we enter a second corridor that splits into two ends. Gloria is waiting on the right.

"Right on time," she chimes and walks over to us. My heart drops a little.

"Have you ever known me to be late?" It's not quite a grumble.

"Not once, Adrian." She smiles at him.

"How long do you need?"

Gloria looks me up and down. "Ten minutes?"

"Okay."

He walks off to the left and leaves me with Gloria, who grabs the wheelchair and rolls me in the opposite direction. Before I have time to ask, we enter a change room. Lockers and benches line the walls.

"What's going on?"

"He didn't tell you?"

I shake my head and I can see the smile spread across her lips. "Hydrotherapy."

"What?"

"Let's get you ready. Can you stand up?"

I grit my teeth together, annoyance slithering inside me. "I'm sick of everyone treating me like a child."

Gloria's eyebrow shoots up and she folds her hands across her chest. "Well then, stop acting like one. The longer you take the less time you will have in your session, the more time you get to spend in this hospital with me being treated like a child and not being independent."

I huff and reach for the metal rail along the wall, then stand. Gloria reaches behind me and unbuckles my brace, then reaches for my gown that falls open and slips from my body, gathering at my hands. She reaches for my underwear and peels it from me. I gasp and she chuckles.

"Darlin', I do this all day long, you have nothing I haven't seen before. I'm just helping you change."

"Into what?"

"This."

She holds up a small bikini.

"Where did you get that?"

"Your fiancé brought it in." She doesn't elaborate but starts slipping it onto me weaving her hand through my arms and around my neck through my legs and thighs.

"There." She grabs the gown and pulls it back up. "Okay, let's go."

"Where?" We meander through a short tunnel and emerge on the other side. Adrian stands by the pool, waiting.

Hydrotherapy.

"Here she is." Her voice sings as we approach Adrian.

"Thanks, Gloria."

"When should I be back?"

"An hour."

"Okay."

Without another word, she turns around and leaves, and then we are alone.

The room feels too hot, and the chlorine smell is overbearing. The water reflects off the wall in strange, light blue patterns.

"Can you stand up for me, Tove?" Adrian stretches out his arms and I grab onto him. His hands are soft and strong, and I have to stop myself from throwing myself into him. He leads me to the edge of the pool, and I lean against the cold metal frame. It's wet and slippery.

"Are you ready, Tove?" His savage voice makes my body coil.

"For what?" I whisper.

Adrian reaches for my gown and I freeze as he pushes the fabric away from my body, letting it gather at my hands.

"No!" It a strangled choke, but it's too late, he has seen it. My body, with its collection of new scars and blemishes, all laid bare before him. My breathing quickens and I grip the fabric to my body. "Don't look at me."

His hands cover mine. "It doesn't matter."

"It does to me. I'm a monster." I clutch the fabric closer, wishing I could disappear.

Adrian sighs and his jaw twitches, then he grips the hem of his long-sleeved swimming shirt and rips it from his body.

I gasp.

I can't help looking. His beautiful sculpted torso is covered with long scars, that slice into his otherwise perfect skin. My eyes travel along the long, deep blemish that rounds his shoulder, and the jagged rough scar that rounds his hip to the sharp tip of a scar that peeks from his shorts and hugs snugly that perfect V that lines his raked abdomen.

"Have you seen enough?"

I unglue my eyes from his body and find his face. "I'm sorry, I didn't mean to…"

"Now we can both be monsters."

My eyes fall away, and I am flooded with guilt. There is something tortured in his voice, an old anguished pain. But also, something else, deep inside of me I feel a flutter of something warm and familiar.

Adrian's firm grip tightens around me as we waddle into the pool. The water is warm and Adrian manoeuvres me until all but my shoulders are submerged. I feel weightless.

"Hold on to the wall with one hand."

I do as he says.

He stands behind me and all I can feel is the water lapping in the inch of space between us.

"Lift up your leg, stretch then put it down again."

I lift up my leg and do as I was told.

"What happened to you?" I ask.

The silence behind me steals away my nerves. "I'm sorry I shouldn't have…'

"I fell," he finally says.

"You fell?"

"I fell out of a window."

My right leg drives up and down, pushing against the water. The world slows down as my left foot slips from beneath me and then loses contact with the floor. A spike of fear shoots through me as for a second I am floating, falling, sinking. I tumble back against Adrian's solid chest and claw at his arms. He grabs me by the waist, muscular arms close around me, holding me firm.

He says nothing as I find the safety of the floor, readjust, regroup, but his hands remain on my waist, and I want them there. They burn through my skin, it tingles and aches and I find myself pushing back, further into him. I want to feel all of him all over me.

"Are you okay, Tove?"

My heart churns as his hot breath tickles my ear. "I think so."

"Good. Now keep working." His grip tightens.

I gasp and find my voice. "How do you fall out of a window?"

I raise my leg and each time I do, I sink deeper into Adrian, his fingers tighten their grip on me, digging into my flesh. I turn my head, pressing my cheek against his torso, memorising every jagged edge, every white broken streak of skin knitted together so harshly. I inhale him, his earthy, forest smell embedded into him as if he's just rolled around in a bed of freshly dewed grass. He sucks in a sharp breath and exhales with a groan, a shudder ripples through me as his fingers clench deeper into my skin.

"I saw a monster."

"A monster?" I swallow hard.

"It turned out to be the most beautiful girl I've ever known."

I can't find air. Adrian's creeping heat closes around me. "What happened to her?"

"She was also the ugliest."

His voice cracks and my throat constricts as his pain leaks into the pool, staining the water around us.

"Adrian..."

"Tove." His breath tickles my ear with his low timber voice, and I can hear need and desire in it, thick and delicious and agonised. "Lift your leg higher."

"I can't." I whimper against him when all I want to do is melt into him.

A hand slips away from my waist and fingers trace my flesh, closing around my thigh. Another creeps around me, drawing me against him. My breathing falters as his breath whispers along my shoulder and his light stubble grazes my cheek.

We are locked together. He says nothing as he guides my leg, pushing and sliding through the water.

Up.

Down.

Up.

Down.

His body pushes against me, and his breath burns my skin, my heart wants to tear itself from my rib cage.

Adrian is everywhere, he's like a buzzing living thing inside of me, my whole body is flooded with the need for him. I push against him and he groans into my neck, "Tove…" and I can hear the breaking point. It's strained and thin and if I push just a little harder maybe I could tip him over the edge.

The air thickens around us, it rolls down my throat and coats my insides with Adrian. He brings with him a hurricane. I can feel the beginnings of it. It will usher destruction and devastation. The water ripples between us and his body presses against mine, his hard cock digging into my flesh. The water no longer soothing, but a murky soup doused with uncertain emotion and clear desire.

"Adrian…" My hands ache for him, my body screaming with need.

His silence twists around me. His hand slips away from my leg and clenches my waist, his velvety hands harsh and demanding, sinking into my flesh. The other slides along my skin, leaving a searing trail, then grips my thigh. Again, we dance against one another.

A wild puppet master wields all the power, bending my body to his will. His lips graze my neck, a whisper of sensation. I feel it everywhere, like a hot wind.

"Adrian–" The voice is not mine, it's dark and heated and is asking for things neither of us should be doing.

His hands tighten around me, gathering me into him, he buries his head into the curve of my neck and his teeth nip at my skin. He inhales me, and my heart clenches with want. Adrian utters a pained groan before his grip falls away and he steps back. The spell is broken, the hurricane passing by without ever hitting ground.

"I'm sorry." His voice is strained and his heat seeps from me as the water spilling between us drains it away from my body. "I shouldn't have…"

He rushes from the water like a tsunami, grabs his shirt, covers up his broken torso, then comes back and fishes me from the water. He wraps a towel around me, and my body shivers at his touch.

His gaze locks with mine and I can see he is searching for something. Whatever he is about to say is swallowed by Gloria's sing-song voice as she comes tumbling from the change room.

Adrian grabs a towel and scrubs it across his face, breaking the tension between us.

"How was your session, T?"

"Good, thanks," I say, not looking at Adrian,

"Well, you must have worked hard. You're all flushed."

I feel the heat rise to my face and I don't dare look up. "I did."

"Well let's get you dry and dressed."

"Thanks."

"Good work today, Tove." His voice slices through my heart. "See you tomorrow."

"See you tomorrow, Adrian." My voice clips and I catch myself too late as Gloria wheels me into the change rooms.

Adrian

*F*uck, *fuck, fuck.*

That was a mistake. I stand under the hot shower trying to wash away my sins. Revenge is not meant to feel like this. It should be cold and hard and twisted. Instead it feels soft, and smells like watermelon. I try to find the anger that shimmers beneath my skin, the resentment, I want to drown in it so that I can drown away these other feelings.

The lines I crossed are all sorts of wrong, but fuck, feeling Tove against me was all sorts of right. My body remembered every inch of hers. It lit up in ways that have been dormant for years.

Her heat sets me alight, and I want to flow over her like molten lava, cover every part of her with every inch of me. I want to make her moan again. The sound, like a delicious melody, is forever engraved into my soul. Familiar and new all at once. A wild hungry tune that my fingers write with her body, for my ears only.

I should have stopped. I should have pulled away, but I couldn't. She's under my skin like an addiction. I need to quit, but I just need one more hit.

I wrench a hand through my wet locks and hit the wall with an open palm. Everything has twisted on its head. I can't do this to her. Shouldn't. I know she deserves it. Every agonising, painful thing I have planned for her, but fuck it, I am and have always been totally and completely in love with Tove Savage.

I grab my swollen cock and slide a soapy hand along the shaft, my eyes slam shut as I hear her moans. I groan through clenched teeth, and my body splinters apart.

I haul in a frayed breath.

Tove

Strange vivid dreams plague me. A monster mask, a beautiful boy falling through the air, a crushed rose, angry shouts. Doctors Jäger assures me the dreams are my memories trying to barge through the wall I've erected. I would have rather dreamt of Adrian. He's all I can think about even as Tray sits by my bed and talks.

He comes every day now, but I don't ever hear him. He talks at me and his words fall away against the wall of my mind. I should give him a chance, I know I should, but despite the niceties and flowers and endless stories, as soon as he leaves my room, he is as forgettable as my other memories.

I look at the clock, three

Two

One.

"Good morning Tove." His voice glides over Tray as if he isn't in the room. Tray stands up and the two men exchange a hostile look.

"See you later, babe," Tray coos and grabs my head,

cupping it between his hands. He presses his lips to mine and parts my lips with a swipe of his tongue. He tastes like stale coffee and regret.

His gaze locks with a brooding Adrian as he leaves the room.

I wipe my mouth with the back of my hand and I'm already pushing myself up. Adrian's lips twitch with a phantom smile.

"How many steps today?" I ask.

"Today we are getting out of this room."

My heart flickers at the thought, but there's no wheel-chair and I know we won't be going to the pool again. Not after…

I brush a hand through my hair, trying to rake the memory away. "Where are we going?"

"Out."

"Doctor Adrian, are you asking me on a date?"

He bites his full lower lip and my heart somersaults into my throat. "You're burning daylight Savage," he quips but doesn't say no.

I reach for my beanie and slide it over my head, the raw, fresh scar still red and angry slithering across my forehead and wrapping itself behind my right ear.

"How do I look?" I pull the beanie to the edge of my eyebrows.

"Ravishing, as always." His pensive face gives nothing away and I am left to wonder if he was joking or not. I swallow and grab onto my walking frame.

We walk. Adrian walks and I amble alongside him like a wounded deer.

We exit the room and pass the nurses' station and continue down the corridor. We have walked these corridors before, lap after lap, building my strength, my confidence. Today Adrian leads me away from our usual route and towards a set of double doors.

I can smell cooked egg and bacon and the undeniable aroma of fresh brewed coffee. Adrian opens the door for me, and the smell is like a wall. I walk through it, enveloped by the smell of humanity. Food and perfume and clinging ashen cigarette smoke. It hits me all at once, so familiar, so foreign.

I grip my beanie and pull it lower over my eyes as we step inside a cafeteria.

"I didn't know this was here," I mumble, taking it all in.

The cafeteria is a cacophony of loud chatter, which drills against my skull. Tables tossed around the room are surrounded by huddles of people, raising their voices to be heard above the din. Colourful food lines the fridges and clashes with the simple décor. Light spills into the room through floor to ceiling windows, washing everyone in a yellow hue. My head spins and I grab onto Adrian.

He leads me to a table with hard plastic chairs and helps me ease into one. "Are you okay?" The concern is back in his green eyes and I want to wipe away his fears.

"Fine." I nod and fidget with my beanie. "Just a little overwhelmed."

He nods and scratches a hand across his chin. "Would you like to go back to your room?"

"No. I think I'd like a coffee."

"Coffee?" He cocks his head and an eyebrow shoots up.

"You promised me a date," I tease.

His mouth falls slightly open then his lips curl into a sly smile that threatens to suck the air from my lungs.

"This isn't a date, Tove. Just coffee." The way he says my name makes my spine ripple.

"Okay." I shrug.

His forehead creases before he turns away.

I watch as he swaggers to the counter and gets us two cups. He sets the coffee on the table and sits down.

"Well done, that was a long walk." He takes a long sip and I watch as his thick lips close around the plastic.

"Thanks, I feel stronger."

"You look it. You should be getting out of here soon." His grip tightens against his coffee cup.

"Unlikely."

He shoots me a questioning look.

Emotion slithers up my throat. "Doctor Jäger won't release me."

"Your memory?"

I nod and ignore the hot tears pooling in my eyes. "My dad had some '*work emergency*' which probably means he didn't want to have to look after me, so he's gone—"

"Tove..."

"No, it's okay." I swallow the sob that threatens to spill from me. "I don't want to be released to Tray, he still feels like a stranger. And nothing is working, my memories just refuse to surface."

"They will come." He sounds so sure, I want to believe him.

"Sometimes I feel like I can catch a thread of something, and my mind chases it like a dog after a car, but the car is too fast and I'm just a broken dog..." My chest constricts.

Adrian's fingers twitch around his coffee cup.

"Give it time."

I roll my eyes. "I have, I even did all the stupid things Doctor Jäger suggested. But it's no use."

"What things?"

"Like repeating information I want to remember, or writing things down in a notebook." My ears burn with the memories of what I've written, and I suck on my coffee to hide the rising flush of my cheeks and silly grin about to rip itself across my face.

I feel eyes on us. On him. I scan the room, Adrian pretends not to notice the eyes glued to his face, whispers and fingers flying about as he becomes the main subject of conversation on every other table.

He notices me noticing. "Don't worry about it."

I adjust my beanie. "Does it ever stop?"

His eyes slide across my beanie and he shrugs. "Give it ten minutes, they will get it out of their system. Then they get bored with the freak show and move on to something else."

I can see the hint of sadness as it passes like a cloud inside his eyes. "Is that how you feel? Like a freak?"

"Sometimes."

My heart splinters at his anguish.

"And other times?"

He sucks in a long breath and puts his coffee on the table. "Other times, I remind myself that beauty is a socially constructed notion, by an industry that makes people feel shit about themselves."

"Does that work?"

He shrugs and his lips curl, pulling at his face in both directions. "I might be the ugliest person in this room, but I guarantee you, that everyone here goes home and finds something to hate about themselves. My..." he gestures around his face, "issues, are just more obvious."

My hands flutters at the edge of my beanie and, without thinking, I rip it from my head and set it on the table, tucking my hair behind my ears.

The gasps are audible, and the looks are blatant, but it's Adrian's eyes that capture mine. Wide and awed.

He clears his throat. "You don't have to do that."

"It can't be a freak show with only one freak."

"Tove—"

"I need to do this, for me, too."

We drink the rest of the coffee in silence. Adrian broods in that way of his, giving me nothing. When we stand to go, the man at the table next to us stares. His finger waves and his eyes lock on Adrian's face. Judging, disgusted, fearful.

"Take a fucking picture. It will last longer!" I call to the man who flinches and recoils like a snail into his seat.

When we exit the cafeteria, Adrian is smiling. "You enjoyed that, didn't you?"

"So much." I laugh.

"You didn't have to do that either."

"I wanted to." My hand slips into his and he freezes. Adrian spots a door, pushes it open and drags me inside, locking the door behind us.

"You can't just do that," he growls. His towering shape looms over me, his entire body heaving with breath. I retreat till my back hits the wall.

"What? Tell people not to look at you?" My eyes focus on his mouth.

"No."

My pulse skitters. "Then what?"

"Grab my hand like that."

"Why not?" My skin heats as it radiates from him. Being this close to Adrian makes me want to burst into flames.

He wrenches a hand through his hair and his face looks torn. "I work here, Tove, and this," he gestures with his hand between us, "it needs to stop."

"What if I don't want it to stop?" I trace his sharp, angular, jaw as it tenses.

"Tove…" he growls in warning. One I don't want to heed.

I snake my hands around his neck and pull him closer, his expression darkens, his eyes full of longing and desire. He raises a hand towards me, only to curl it into a fist that slams into the wall by my head.

"I don't want it to stop," I whisper against his mouth. I push up on my tiptoes and our lips crash against one another. He groans a desperate hungry sound, low in his throat, and then his arms circle me, drawing me closer.

I taste the coffee on his lips. My breathing hitches as his hand slithers up my back, creeping fingers tracing my skin. His body pins me against the wall, pushing into me, and he kisses me harder. His hands tighten around me, pulling me against him.

My hands find his back and my nails dig into his skin. He groans against my mouth and I swallow the raw carnal need, which rushes through my body like wildfire.

His lips are warm and soft, and possessive and urgent. He grips my hair and tilts my head back, deepening the kiss, our connection. We are a closed circuit in the midst of a power surge, electricity flies unchecked in all directions.

We are greedy. We both search for more. Need more, want more. I cling to Adrian desperately. I feel him everywhere, and it's almost too much. He edges his thumb along the curve of my breast. I moan into his mouth, and he breaks away.

Adrian releases me slowly, his hands fall away, as if he is reluctant to let me go. He draws in a frayed breath.

"We— I shouldn't have—" he strains, but there is hard desperation behind his words, an aching need that echoes my own.

'I'm sorry." My lips burn. I'm not sorry at all.

Our eyes lock in a losing battle of need and denial. Adrian's face is a mask cut in half, confusion and anger on one side, regret and sadness on the other.

"Take me to my room." I lick my lips and my heart churns in my chest, the last fluttering butterfly falling to the empty pit of my stomach with clipped wings.

He nods and cracks the door open. His body presses against me as he checks the corridor, I hear his heart slam inside his chest, his body a furnace. The door flings open and he ushers me to the corridor where we walk the rest of the way in silence that feels like a pregnant woman about to give birth. Waves of contractions flow between us, unsaid words and hard-hitting emotions and yet we say nothing.

When we walk into the room, Tray is sitting on the edge

of the bed. His gaze flickers from Adrian to me then back again and his lips curl.

"Where have you been?" His voice is clipped and agitated.

"My morning walk, same as every day at this time."

He stares at Adrian as he talks to me. "Do you always take this long?"

"Rehabilitation is different with everyone –"

"I wasn't talking to you," he growls at Adrian, who doesn't flinch.

"Tray! Leave him alone."

"You're defending him?"

Something in the back of my mind ticks, it's like a pull deep inside me. I try and hold on to the wisp, but it flutters away like smoke in the wind.

"Can you leave, please?"

"Are you serious?" Tray's face is flushed and his head swivels between Adrian and me. "What the fuck, Tove?"

"I believe she asked you to leave."

"Stay out of it, freak." The words cut through the room like a knife and I feel the wound he inflicted on Adrian as if he sliced my skin.

"Tray." I hissed through clenched teeth and his gaze flickers back to me. "Leave."

"Are you serious?"

"Now."

His jaw clenches and his face curdles like old milk. He storms out of the room, leaving behind charged electricity. It bounces off the walls without an outlet.

I suck in a deep breath and settle my aching heart. Was I really going to marry that man?

"Are you okay?" Adrian's honey voice cuts through the terror.

"Yes."

"Are you sure?"

His gaze holds mine and the forest in his eyes is full of turmoil and despair.

"Yes. Are you?"

He shrugs and turns to leave.

"Adrian?"

"Yeah?"

"Were you someone to me? Before?"

"See you tomorrow, Tove."

FIVE WEEKS AFTER THE ACCIDENT

Tove

Tray's mouth is moving but I haven't heard a word he's said for the last five minutes. I think it's something to do with how important he is, or his job, or him at his job. It's just that I feel indifferent. I look into his eyes and all I find is a vast emptiness, like a desert, they're nothing like the forest green of Adrian. My body shivers as I think of him. The name makes my tongue flicker as though I've just tasted something familiar but unusual, a unique flavour that's so rare I could never forget it, and yet I have.

Tray is still talking his voice grinds against me and I wish he'd stop.

And then he does.

My eyes focus on his lips. They twitch in irritation or maybe anticipation.

"Tove. Did you hear me?"

"Yeah, of course."

"So, what do you say?"

I bite the inside of my cheek, wondering if I could backtrack and admit I didn't hear a word he said. But then I'm gripped with fear that he might start all over again.

I try a safe option. "Okay."

"Okay? Great!" He seems genuinely happy and dread sinks in. What the fuck did I just do?

"Thank you so much for giving me another chance. I know I was out of line, the other day."

I nod, still confused. How did we get here? I was going to ask him to stop coming. Instead he is beaming at me like I just handed him the sun.

"I'll go clear it up with Doctor Jäger before we leave. I'll even bring that dress you love."

I have a dress? I wonder but I can't ask him because he's already across the yard, running back inside.

I stand abandoned, looking at the daunting task before me. Yes, I've walked this distance twice before, but it was exhausting, and I've never done it alone. I feel vulnerable. I should have never agreed to come out here with Tray.

I pinch my eyes shut and wonder if we were really ever happy. Or maybe I was just a different person before the accident.

I take a small step and my heart is gripped with panic. There are too many steps.

"Prince Charming forgot his princess." The warm dark voice slithers around me and the panic melts away.

"He's just excited, I guess."

Adrian steps beside me and offers me his arm. I give him a questioning look and his head cocks in silent approval. I grip his arm and feel the flex and pull of every muscle. Heat rushes to my face as my body recalls the hardness of his body, colliding with mine.

"Let's get you back inside." His free hand closes around mine, and a shiver climbs up my not so broken spine.

"Don't you want to know why he's excited? "

"Not really." His usual warm voice holds an icy edge.

"I think he's taking me out." I feel the jerk of his muscles around me. There's a momentary stillness and then he takes another step as if nothing at all had happened.

"He's not my patient." He shrugs. "Are you excited? "

My heart bounces around my chest like a loose ball. "I don't know."

"Oh?" His grip tightens, his fingers digging into my skin.

"I don't know. Maybe we were happy. Maybe those feelings are right there just beneath all this fog, waiting for me to feel them again."

He's stiffer than before, his fluid muscles rigid. He pushes a hand through his thick hair. We pause, his eyes clutching to mine. They're a deep dark forest I could lose myself in. Tumble over roots and lie on the moss-covered earth till it was all I could breathe.

"And if they are, do you want to feel them again?"

I bite my lip and fall into his eyes. Do I want to feel anything for Tray at all?

I open my mouth, doubt about to spill out, but Tray bursts out of the building and ploughs into us, his momentum pushing me off my feet.

In a swift movement Adrian catches me, holding me tightly against him. His strong arms caging me, his earthy dangerous scent envelopes me and his heart slams in my ears. Or maybe it's mine.

"Are you all right?" he asks, just as Tray straightens and frowns.

"Watch where you're going." His tone is icy cold.

Adrian doesn't acknowledge him. "Are you all right, Tove?" he asks again.

"Yeah, I think so."

His grip loosens and instantly I miss the heat of his body as Tray yanks me away.

"Doctor Jäger cleared you for dinner." He beams and my

ears burn as I feel Adrian's eyes on the back of my neck. He hasn't moved at all.

I force a smile at Tray's direction. And he turns his attention back to Adrian. "You are dismissed. I'll get her to her room."

I shudder inwardly at the words and feel the cool space as it freezes over between the two men that stand on either side of me.

Adrian turns to me. "Enjoy your dinner." His warm tone feels chilly as he walks towards the hospital door.

"What a freak." Tray shakes his head.

"You should be kinder to people, he was only doing his job."

"Was he now?"

"What's your problem?"

"What's yours? Do you have something for that freak?"

"Don't be ridiculous, he's just my physio."

"Yeah he is, and he shouldn't take advantage of you in your vulnerable state."

I bite my lip. Is that what Adrian is doing to me? Taking advantage? Except that Adrian is the one that keeps pushing me away.

"You're being paranoid."

"Don't talk to me like that." He spits then recovers, brushing his hand over his face. "Look Tove, I'm sorry, but what do you expect? I've almost lost you once. I don't know what I'd do if I'd lost you again."

He takes my hand in his and pulls it to his mouth, laying a gentle kiss on the back of it. "Sorry."

"No, I am. I just forget that you have all this history with me and..."

"It's okay, just— forget it, let's get you upstairs and get some rest. I'll drop the dress off later so you can get ready."

I nod and let him lead me to the elevator bank, fighting

the urge to look around and search the lobby. I feel his eyes on me. I know he is watching.

❧

I stare out the window and watch Tray walk down the trail towards his car. He is talking on his phone and seems to be fighting with someone. He stops and his hand slices through the air, then his face flushes. I see him sigh in surrender and he nods.

The call ends and he stuffs the phone into his pocket. Whatever was said made him jittery, because he slams the door shut and his car screeches away.

I stare at the empty parking space for a while. Do I really love this man as much as he says? Everyone keeps telling me my memories will come back and I can feel them, they are trying to push through. I can almost feel the pressure of them ramming against my skull, filtering into every empty space and cavity. I want them to burst that dam but as hard as I try, they won't come.

I know Doctor Jäger says the accident has changed me, but surely not so much that I don't even know myself.

I exhale and switch the TV on, hoping something mindless will bring me out of my funk.

❧

At four o'clock there's a knock on the door.

Tray walks in without waiting for me to answer.

"Hey beautiful," he says as he walks over to the bed. His eyes trace my scar, he slows and plants a tentative kiss on my cheek.

I don't feel beautiful, in fact, I've been avoiding the mirror as much as I can.

I sense the scars on my face. Thick heavy skin loops and

gnashes at my forehead. I lurch away from him. If he notices he doesn't say anything.

He unfolds a black dress on the bed. It looks tiny, one thin strap and barely enough material to cover my body.

I eye the thing like a corpse on the bed.

"It was your favourite...from before..." He clears his throat and his eyes take a lengthy hungry trip along my body. "Try it on."

"I'm going to need some help." I grab the fabric and try to work out how it might stretch across enough of me.

"I'm right here." He sucks on his lower lip.

"You need to get out." I flick my eyes to the door.

"But Tove, I've seen you naked." His voice is low and husky, and that flash is back in his eyes.

I wring my hands around myself. He hasn't seen my new body yet. I cringe inwardly.

"I don't remember that."

He frowns as if I'm using my memory loss as an excuse to keep distance between us.

Maybe I am.

He pouts, then relents. "I'll be just outside."

"Can you call Gloria?"

"What for?"

"So she can zip me up." I glare at the 'dress' on my bed and bile coats the inside of my throat.

"I can help you with that." He has that hungry grin on his face, and I shake my head.

"Just get Gloria, please."

His shoulders slump and irritation etches his features for a second. Or maybe it's disappointment. I can't tell.

The door swings open and Gloria steps inside.

Tray is holding the handle and his eyes sweep over me, as though what is standing before him is not good enough. Not beautiful enough. Not perfect enough. My fingers flinch to my scar.

I shake away the uncertainty that's building inside of me, the doubt.

"Tray says you need some help, T?"

"Yeah, he's brought in my favourite dress?"

It comes out as a question.

Gloria's face crinkles as she looks at it. "This was your favourite?"

"That's what he says." I shrug. I look at the dress, uncertainty flowing through me.

"We're gonna make you look gorgeous, T." Gloria smiles at me and tugs at my pyjamas. "Come on, time to turn some heads." She giggles and I get swept away by the sound.

I roll my eyes and pull my clothes off, not looking down. I know what's down here, I don't want to see it again.

Adrian saw. He didn't care. My heart twitches at the thought of him.

"You're going to have to take that off too." She nods at my bra and I sigh.

I reach over and discard the bra. Gloria brings the dress over and waits for me to squeeze inside. The stretchy material is so tight it feels suffocating. I feel exposed, naked. There's not enough fabric. There's too much skin, too much scarring.

The dress rests just below my ass and the single strap is barely holding it up, accentuating the swell of my naked breasts. My cold nipples pebble and rub against the material. I shudder at the sensation, squeezing my thighs together.

"Well, it's a perfect fit." Gloria whistles and I ignore her while trying to adjust into my new skin.

"Let's take care of your face now." She smiles and produces a small compact from her bag.

I stare at the makeup, tears brimming in my eyes.

I sit down and let Gloria smear foundation on my face, layer after layer. I feel the liquid fill in the cavities, erase the imperfections, the tragedy. She takes her time, slow and meticulous as she is with everything she does. Gloria brushes my hair, pulling and raking through my wild mane, taming it.

She paints my lips and looks at me, her handiwork, her masterpiece.

"He's going to have a hard time keeping his hands off you." She winks at me and nods towards the bathroom. "Go look."

I edge to the bathroom door and push it open, then freeze on the threshold. My heart thuds in my chest as my heartbeat spikes. I want to be brave, but I'm just a coward. I've been avoiding the mirror. If I don't see them, maybe they don't exist. A sliver of a pang shoots through me, as if maybe that's something I've said or heard *before*. I wait to see if more will come, but it doesn't.

"Go on T, he's waiting for you."

I flick the lights on and take a long breath before stepping into the bathroom. I find my reflection in the mirror and my breath stumbles, my pounding heart smashing against my rib cage.

I stare at the woman staring back me. She is flawless and beautiful, and I want to be her again. Flitting fingers of guilt thread through me. I could step off the freak show bus. I could be just like *before*. Just like everyone else. Everyone but him.

The tears come back and Gloria appears by my side. "Don't cry now, or you'll ruin it."

I step closer to the mirror and examine my face, turning it back and forth in a frantic pendulum.

"Gloria." I swallow back tears, unable to make words come out.

I swivel my head, scrutinising the skin, searching for the deep scars, but they are gone, hidden behind the mask.

I reach for Gloria and she gathers me into her arms, giving me a tight hug.

"Go have fun, T, you deserve it."

She smiles at me and I can feel the affection, it's motherly. My heart pangs as I wonder about my own mother. I've read about her in my notes. I remember what my father told me. I think I miss her. I wish they were real memories.

I clear my head, not wanting those thoughts to cloud my date with Tray.

Gloria opens the door for me and I step through.

Tray gasps as he sees me, his hand reaching for mine. "Wow, you look gorgeous." He brings my knuckles to his mouth and lands a sweet kiss on them.

"Let's go, we don't have much time. Doctor Jäger was very clear about your curfew." An edge of annoyance laces his voice.

He leads us to the elevator bank and we wait. When the door opens, Adrian is leaning against the back wall of the elevator. His gaze leaves his phone and his eyes grow wide as he sees me. He isn't wearing his usual scrubs but a tight-fitting long-sleeved shirt that shows off his muscular physique and low hanging jeans that look like they were moulded for his body.

I go to step inside and Tray pulls me back, wrapping a hand around my shoulders. "We'll take the next one."

Adrian's eyes burn into mine, not even acknowledging Tray. There's fire there and hunger and wild unreserved passion and I can feel it like a wave pushing through the elevators, flooding the entire corridor, saturating every part of me.

The elevator door snaps shut and I'm sure I hear a distant growl.

"You're being ridiculous, Tray," I say.

"I don't trust him."

"I don't know what you're seeing that I'm not."

"I don't like the way he looks at you, like a monster that wants to eat you."

"That's a strange thing to say." I have to hold my voice from quivering and my knees from buckling. The idea of Adrian eating me seems way too appealing.

I shake the thought away and squeeze Tray's hand. "Well, I'm here with you so obviously there's nothing for you to worry about."

He tips his head and smiles, but I feel the tension still in his body, in the way his hand clutches mine. Tightly. Possessively.

We wait for the next elevator and head downstairs. Tray leads me through the lobby and towards the back of the hospital where the resident gardens bloom.

"Where are we going?"

"Shh, just wait."

We walk through the garden and then I see it. A single table sits in the middle of the garden. A white cloth hides the plastic beneath. The table is laid with plates, glasses and a pitcher of water. Fairy lights twinkle in the bushes, illuminating the dark garden.

"It's lovely."

Tray holds a chair out for me, and I sit down, giggling.

He smiles at me, and his face relaxes for the first time that day. He looks younger, like a version of himself he doesn't often show.

"You went all out," I say, looking at the foodless table.

"But wait, there's more." He puts on a show master voice and I giggle as he pulls a sealed plastic box from under the table. He opens it steam escapes from within. He pulls out take-away containers with meat, rice and noodles.

"Thai, it's your favourite."

"Is it?" I eye the food and my stomach growls. Maybe it remembers something I don't.

Tray grunts and pulls out a second box. From it he produces a bottle of Champagne. I look at the green bottle and then at Tray.

"You know I can't drink."

"Just a taste… it's a special occasion."

"Tray…"

He ignores me and pours us each a glass. More than a taste.

He sits down, pulling his chair closer to mine.

"Help yourself." He grabs one of the containers and piles a generous amount of rice onto his plate.

"Which one should I try first?"

"Any of them."

"But which one did I like best?"

He looks at me as if I have asked him for the square root of 3691693 and then sighs. "All of it, Tove, you love all of it."

"Okay." I feel the disappointment wash over me.

I dish some food onto my plate and shovel a forkful onto my mouth. The delight is instantaneous. I don't need to be told I love this food, my tongue remembers already. The tingle and burn of the chili, the sharp bite of the lemon, the sticky rice – it's as if my mouth is alive and my body is celebrating. I wait for my brain to catch up, for the lightbulb to switch on, but it doesn't.

Tray holds up his glass, bubbles rising along the plastic. "Cheers, baby." He waits.

"Tray, you know –"

"Come on, babe, don't leave me hanging. It's one drink."

I sigh and grab the glass. "Cheers." I gulp and the Champagne explodes in my mouth.

Tray chuckles. It's a lovely sound and despite the fact that he is laughing at me, I like it. It's the first time I've heard it. It's smooth and carefree, nothing like the heavy savagery in Adrian. I bat the thought away and wipe my chin.

"Tell me more about things I like."

The question seems to take him by surprise. His eyes widen and he chews slowly, thinking, digesting as he lets his fork drop.

"Like what?"

"Like, do I like cats or dogs?"

"Dogs."

"Really?"

"Of course."

"Do I, we, have one?"

"Not yet, but we did talk about getting one after the wedding. As practice."

"Practice?"

"Yeah, for our kids?"

"Kids?"

"Yes, three, remember?"

"No." I shake my head and an awkward silence washes over us.

I clear my throat.

"What about friends? Do I have a best friend?"

"Yeah, me." He flashes some teeth and his dimples come out and he looks so handsome and playful, I start to see the reasons I might have fallen for him.

"Tell me about my photography studio."

"Not much to tell, people come, you click, they leave."

"Oh." My heart sags. I clear my throat and try a different route. "What about you, Tray? What do you like?"

His body swivels towards me and he looks to my eyes.

"You, Tove, I like you." His hand lands on my naked thigh and I shiver beneath him.

"I like touching you, Tove." His fingers trail the length of my thigh, my eyes flicker from his hand to his face, but I am frozen in place, my heart chugging in my chest.

"I like how you taste." He leans in and I gasp as his lips brush my neck. He peppers kisses along the long column of my neck and trails my collar bone.

"I like how your lips feel on mine," he whispers, as he clamps my mouth with his, fusing us in a kiss. His hand finds the back of my head and threads through my hair and he tugs slightly, lifting my mouth to his.

His lips are soft and the kiss feels like a trickle, not a flood. It fizzles out like a cold shower, the electricity somehow missing the fuse. It's sweet and nothing else. Like a singular flavour. There is nothing to unravel in your mouth, no multitude of layers or tastes, just one monotone.

He pulls away and searches my eyes. Maybe he's looking for that spark, or maybe for permission, because his hand travels up my waist and my breast is in his large hand.

"I've missed you, Tove." His hot breath is at my ear and he buries his head in my neck and dips down to my chest. My head spins as his hot mouth picks at the swells of my breast.

A chill trickles up my spine, a familiar primal fear, my entire body screaming at me, a memory inked into my skin that my mind will not recollect. I try to settle my hammering heart and control my breathing, it's shallow and comes in in short sharp bursts.

Tray's hands explore my body and my mouth is clamped shut. I want to ask him to stop, to breathe, but he captures my hand in his and puts it on his hard cock. "See, Tove?" His voice is raspy. "See what you do to me?"

His mouth slams against mine and he closes my hand around his hard shaft, moving it up and down. "I want you, Tove, I've been waiting for you for so long. Tell me you want me too." He brushes my lips with his own. "Tell me Tove, just say yes."

I flinch at the words and he freezes. His posture stiffens for a microsecond, long enough for me to notice it. Was it something he said?

His eyes scrutinise me for a long moment then he leans in again. I move away from him, denying the kiss.

"I think I want to go upstairs to my room."

"Tove, I—"

"It's too soon." I stand up and push away from him, the

plastic chair falling mutely on the grass. I pull the skirt back down, trying to cover more of my thighs, trying to hide from his hungry eyes.

He pinches the bridge of his nose, closes his eyes and sucks in a long breath. When he opens them again he looks shaken, scared almost.

"You're right, Tove. I'm sorry. I was moving way too fast. Come and sit, let's not let the food go to waste." He stands up and corrects the fallen chair, holding it for me.

My body twists at the thought of food. Food with Tray.

"Sorry, Tray, but I'm tired."

It looks as though he wants to protest, to explode, to implode, instead he nods, his mouth stretched in a severe line. "Let me take you to your room."

"No." I back away. "I think I need some air."

"Tove—"

"It's too much, too fast. Let my body catch up to my brain."

He steps closer. "I know what your body wants, Tove. I've given it plenty of attention in the past." His eyes rove the length of my legs and my swollen breasts that want to explode out of the tight material.

I swallow the rock that's pushing its way up my throat, my head still light. "My body isn't the same." Heat rises to my cheeks and tears pool at my eyes.

"Of course it is, I mean, fucking look at you, you're fucking hot."

I lick my lips, they feel dry. I feel like I haven't drunk anything in years. "*I'm* not the same."

"That's okay, it gives us a chance to get to know each other again, to fall in love all over again." He steps closer. "Do you know how rare that is? How many people get a second chance at love?"

I bite the inside of my cheek, my head spinning. I lose my train of thought. The world blurs.

"Tray…" My voice comes out a weak whisper, and my body feels heavy.

The world tilts and then all I can see is the darkness.

My body wakes up before the rest of me, feeling weighed down by foreign hands. I can hear someone humming to themselves in agreement.

Some of me feels hot and some of me feels cold, and then there are hands again and I don't like them because they shouldn't be there. There are voices. Or maybe it's one voice. It drips over me like melting ice. He's apologetic, he's desperate.

'I'm sorry, I just need the money, you have to understand. You won't remember anything anyway…"

No! My brain screams, it comes out like a muffled and pathetic groan.

"Collateral, for daddy dearest. I have too many debts…"

When I come to, I am sitting on the plastic chair. My chest feels heavy and my head fuzzy.

"Tray?"

He's touching me, did he just pull up my dress?

I feel odd, dirty, afraid.

"Tray, what's happening?"

"I'm just taking care of things, it's okay."

"Things?" my head doesn't want to stay upright.

"The future."

"The future?"

"Our future." He smiles at me but it doesn't touch his eyes. "It will all be okay."

My mouth feels as if I've ingested cotton balls and a mouthful of earth. "Can you take me upstairs, please?"

"Sure thing."

"What happened? How did you take care of things?"

"We just had dinner, we kissed, you liked it. And then you said *yes*." His mouth is spread wide in a grin that feels unnaturally wide.

I look at my hand, where a diamond ring decorates my finger. "I did?"

"Really? You're asking me that?"

"Sorry, I'm just confused. I can't remember anything."

Tray doesn't reply. He yanks me from the chair and holds me up against him. "Don't worry about it, babe."

His mouth closes around mine and I try to push away. His mouth chokes me. I'm light headed. Afraid the world might slip away again.

"Fuck, Tove, I've missed you so much." His forehead leans against mine and his eyes sparkle. I wonder if mine do too, but I don't even have the energy to smile back at him.

"I don't feel well."

"Must be all the excitement. Let me get you to your bed."

He guides me back to my room and lays me on the bed. He says something about a good time and going home tomorrow, but I pass out before I hear anything.

Adrian

My coffee isn't doing its job. Neither did the previous two. My body feels as heavy as my eyelids. Tension locks my jaw coursing inside my body like an underground lake. No matter what I do, the vision of Tove, made up and stunning, being held by that fucker, haunts me. Nothing will ever help. I don't think there's enough alcohol or drugs in the world to numb the pain or erase that image.

I drag the last sip out of the coffee cup and chuck it out. Fuck it, I have to remember why I'm here.

I grit my teeth as I yank on the curtains. As expected, Tove is still in bed, looking groggy and dazed.

My heart pinches at the sight of her. I push the feeling away, reminding myself how much I hate her, but it settles like a fucking parasite and gnaws at my heart.

"Let's go." I scowl through gritted teeth.

"You're a ray of sunshine." She looks ashen.

I take a step closer, leaning over her, scrutinising.

"Are you all right?" *Why the fuck do I care?*

"My head hurts."

"Partied too hard on your *date* last night."

Her face pulls tightly together and her eyes narrow. She bites her lip and avoids my gaze. "I can't remember." It's a tiny whisper, I barely hear it, but it's enough to make every part of me burn with red hot anger. I suck in a long breath, trying to calm myself.

"Maybe it was so boring, you fell asleep." I sniff at her and pull her up to a sitting position. She whines at the movement.

"It wasn't boring." Her eyes flare up.

"Not my business," I snap.

"Isn't it?"

"Why would it be?" I shrug and step closer.

"Really?" Her eyes tear up and I clench my fists tighter, digging the nails into my flesh.

"What you do in your private life, is none of my business, Tove. I am your physiotherapist and nothing more."

Tears pool in her eyes. "What about—"

"Mistakes that should have never happened," I growl.

Her jaw twitches and she bites out at me. "Well, I guess you don't care that he kissed me, or that we made it official."

My nostrils flare and I stand at the foot of the bed, our faces an inch from one another. "Congratulations, I'm sure you'll be very happy together."

Our breaths mingle as her face twists. "Adrian..." My name is laced in hope, desire, wanting. Everything I wanted her to feel for me is in three little syllables. My heart ricochets against my skin. Tove Savage wants me. I can taste it in her breath and see it in the way her body leans closer to mine, the way her eyes beg me to choose her too.

I hold my face steady, schooling my features to remain perfectly still. It's a skill I learned years ago, it's one of the ways I kept my face intact.

I sniff and reach for her leg. "Time for your stretches."

I grab her leg and lift it, stretching the muscles, warming

them up. The tears fall. Silently at first, fat rolls of water that crash against her pillow. And then like an earthquake, her body begins to shiver and crumple. Tove wails. Moans wrench from her throat, pain claws its way out of her.

I've been pining for this day, for four years, wanting to break Tove Savage. I wanted to punish her, to make her hurt, to make her crave me so badly she would rip her own skin off just to feel me against her. But I all of a sudden, I felt the need to re-evaluate the price I was willing to make her pay.

"Tove? Talk to me?"

She shakes her head and wipes away tears that just keep coming.

"*Talk* to me," I growl.

"It's nothing."

I slide my hand under her chin and coax her head up. When our eyes meet, the icebergs in her eyes float in a red sea.

"Tove, what's going on?"

"I'm afraid." She whispers it.

"Of Tray?" I'm almost hopeful.

"No."

"Then what?"

"I can't remember anything."

"But you will."

"No." She clasps my arm, her nails digging into my flesh. "You don't understand. From last night."

"What are you talking about?"

She sucks in a worn breath and another tear leaks down her drawn face. "I remember sitting with him and talking and a kiss and then..." she whimpers, "I don't remember anything."

"Nothing?" The lone tear spatters on my arm.

"What if I'm getting worse? What if I forget everything that's happened since my accident, what if..." She looks into my eyes and my heart drowns in a pool of dread.

"Do you know what day it is?"

"Tuesday?" she asks through a sob.

"And your name?"

"Tove Savage."

"And me?" Fear strokes me with a long black feather.

My hand cups her cheek as our eyes lock.

"Adrian. Adrian Rose."

I nod and consider her words. "Let me call Doctor Jäger, I think you need him today more than you need me."

"No." She grips my hand and her fingers curl around my wrists, her nails slashing into the skin. "I want you to stay."

"Tove."

"*Don't* leave me." Her tears are falling hard and fast and sobs rip from her quaking chest.

"Tove..." My skin burns with her pain. I reach for the call button and Gloria steps inside. At the sight of Tove, her usual casual manner drops away.

"T? Are you all right sweetie?" She approaches us tentatively, her eyes searching my face for answers.

When she is close enough, I turn to Tove. "Tove, Gloria will sit with you while I go get Doctor Jäger. He will check you over and do some tests. You'll be fine."

Slowly, her hands fall away but her eyes remain locked on mine until I leave the room. My heart aches, watching her small frame so agonised.

At the nurses' station I call Dr Jäger's office and leave an urgent message. His secretary will page him, but I know what he will find. Tove is fine, her memory loss has nothing to do with the accident.

I rock up and down on my heels, my fingers jamming the button. I need to get outside. I need to breathe fresh air and clear my head. I need to get away from Tove and her pain before I tear this hospital down brick by fucking brick. The elevator door tears open, and Tray stands inside. He doesn't notice me right away. Not until I lunge at him, blocking his way out. It takes all my will power not to plough a fist though his perfect fucking face.

Our eyes are locked in a raging battle, one our bodies can't have. When the doors close, I rush towards him and twist his shirt in my fist, pinning him against the wall. I'm not the skinny kid he used to beat up. I'm almost twice his size, broader, taller and smarter.

"I know what you did, you fucking asshole."

"What are you talking about?"

"You drugged her."

"You're insane."

"What did you give her, you dick? Rohypnol?"

"What are you talking about?"

"You fucking asshole, you can set her back months! Or maybe that's your plan. She stays here with a broken mind and you get blow jobs in the car park?"

His eyes darken and his face furrows. "Get off me, you freak!"

"Why did you drug her?" I grind out and my fist tightens around his shirt.

"Collateral," he smirks. "In case things don't work out."

"Money?" I let go of his shirt and my fist smashes against the metal wall of the elevator right by his ear. He flinches away as it clangs and pain bursts through my hand.

"You could have fucked everything up."

He shrugs, but I can see fear in his eyes. I won't stay in the hospital forever, and neither will he. "Minor setback at best."

"It doesn't matter how hard you try, she'll get her memory back one day soon, and she'll know everything. In fact – I'm going to go up there right now and tell her everything."

"Are you now?" Suddenly his tone is no longer afraid but cold and malicious. "You do that, and I'm going to tell her who you are, freak."

I still.

"I'll tell her all about you, how you were neighbours. How

you were obsessed with her. Maybe you still are. Are you a stalker? Did you ask for her case? When I'm finished with her, she's never going to want to see you again." He pats his ruffled hair back into place and straightens his shirt. "In fact, I'll make sure you'll never set foot in this hospital again, *freak*. You shouldn't be out in public anyway with that face."

When the elevator doors open again, he pushes by me and saunters out, as a stream of people walk inside. They give me the usual horrified looks as I stand there shedding breath, shaking limbs – in and out, frayed broken breaths. It's time to say goodbye to Tove Savage one last time.

T he air around the stairwell closes in on me, suffocating. My lungs squeeze with effort as I take two stairs at a time. Whether or not I am ready to admit it, I'm afraid of Tray. Not physically. I know I can beat him to a pulp, but I'm wary of what he'll tell Tove, how he might manipulate his words.

I burst through the door of the fourth floor and gather myself. Unease burns my aching muscles and it seems that nothing will settle the quake inside me, the unrelenting wave of uncertainty.

I march down the corridor, my chest squeezing and heavy. I need to get to Tove first. Confess. Absolve myself. Beg for forgiveness.

Tove.

I walk into her room. Doctor Jäger is standing over her bed, her face is tear-streaked and drawn.

They both eye me. The doctor's face is full of concern, Tove's is full of contempt.

"Adrian." His face breaks into a smile. "What are you doing here?"

"I um…" I grip the back of my neck and search for an answer. "I just wanted to make sure you got my message."

"Yes, I did, thank you. You did the right thing calling me."

"Oh, good."

I turn to leave when a body crashes into mine from behind.

"Tove!" Tray runs to her bedside. "I came as soon as I heard."

She flinches away from him, but he pays her no mind. "Are you all right?"

"She is a little shaken up, it seems that the excitement of last night got to her. She did admit to having a drink." The doctor shakes his head and sighs like an exasperated parent. "Perhaps in future we can avoid that?" Dr Jäger cants his head.

"Sorry Doctor, that was my fault, I pushed Tove, you know, so we could celebrate."

"Celebrate?"

"Our engagement." Tray's eyes lift at the sides and he smirks at me. "We made it official last night."

"Indeed. Congratulations, but until Tove gets her memory back there is to be no more alcohol."

Tove nods to herself, her eyes still locked on mine.

"Speaking of her memory," the doctor continues, "I think it's time we try and help Tove a little more."

"How?" Tove's voice is nothing but a scratched whisper.

"Tray and I were talking a few days back and he suggested that you visit your home."

"What?"

"I think it's a good idea, given how far your recovery has come with Adrian here."

"I'm not sure…" she starts but the doctor cuts her off.

"Tove, it's been almost six weeks with no sign of your memory returning. I think it's time we start to use more aggressive methods, or we may have to face facts that this condition might be permanent."

My fists clench together by my sides.

"I'm not sure…" she starts, but this time Tray cuts her off.

"Tove, this is getting ridiculous!"

"What's that exactly?" She glares at him, her voice as glacial as her eyes. "That you are practically still a stranger to me and you want to take me somewhere with you to a place I might not know, to be a stranger in my own life? Which part of that exactly is *ridiculous*? Which part is it that makes the least amount of sense?"

"Tove, that's not what I meant."

They stare at one another, and her eyes seem to glaze over as if she is no longer in the room.

"Tove?" Doctor Jäger calls her with a soft voice. ""I hate to say it, but maybe it's time we stress your system a little, and then see what spills out."

"She needs to come home." Tray talks about her as if she's not in the room. He paces around, like a fox, sly and cunning, making a plan. I see the wheels turning behind his eyes.

He stops, approaches the bed, and reaches for Tove's hand. "Tove? Can you still not remember me? Us?"

"I'm sorry, I just..." She tries to pull away but Tray yanks on her arm.

"Six years can't just be erased overnight, we have a life together!"

Tove snatches her hand from his grip. "I'm sorry." She shakes her head and tears well in her eyes again.

"Will you come home with me? Just to look around? Maybe it will jog your memory, maybe…" His words fall away but I hear the trail of resentment.

Tove bites her lower lip and turns to the doctor. "Doctor Jäger, could someone come with me? From the hospital?"

"I don't think that will be necessary," Tray jumps in.

"Please? I'm going to a stranger's home."

"Tove!" His face turns red as if he's just been punched.

I clench my jaw, fighting the threat of a smile.

"I'm not a stranger, I'm your fucking fiancé!"

"Tray!" The doctor takes a step, inserting himself between Tray and Tove, using his body like a shield. "I think you should wait outside now. We will arrange to transport Tove home. Perhaps it's best if you go ahead, get things— cleaned up."

Silence descends on the room.

Tray runs a twitching hand through his hair and gives me a scalding look as he storms out of the room. His elbow doesn't miss me as he passes the threshold.

Tove turns to me. "Will you come with me?"

My stomach knits at the question. I don't want to see where she lives with that fucker, where she shares her days with him, where she shares her nights with him.

"I don't think that's a goo—"

"That's a perfect idea," the doctor interrupts me mid-protest.

"I…" I shake my head.

"Please?"

Her eyes glisten with unshed tears, the glacier melting inside.

I sigh and draw in a desperate breath. "Okay."

"Fantastic, then it's settled. I'll arrange for a car downstairs." Doctor Jäger is beaming as he leaves to make arrangements.

"Adrian?"

"What?" I snap, and she flinches.

"Thank you."

I scrub my hands over my face and retreat from the room.

～❦～

Tove

Even though my stomach churns and my heart feels as if it might burst from my chest, it's nice to be out of the hospital and away from all the sickness and white walls, from the beeping and food on plastic trays.

I didn't think I would have an issue getting into the car, but it turns out the idea nauseates me. I have no recollection of the accident, just fragments of laughter and the strong smell of alcohol, and yet as soon as I see the car my stomach lurches and I leave a trail of vomit along the white car door.

"It's okay Tove, shhhhh." Adrian's voice strokes my ear as his strong hands hold me up. "It's all going to be okay."

I dry-retch, my stomach knotted and twisted in pain. Adrian holds the hair away from my face and cradles me against him.

"I'm done," I croak.

Silently, Adrian leads me to a bench near the hospital entrance. We sit, the breeze wafting the reeking smell in our direction every so often as if to remind me of my shame.

Everything hurts, my head, my body, my heart. Why am I going to Tray when all I want is to sit here forever with Adrian?

His hands brush mine and I look to his eyes, the forest silent. I edge my hand closer to his and we sit, motionless. His fingers twitch again, and I edge my hand until it is buried beneath his, the heat of his palm pressing against my own. I suck in a frayed breath and, just as I get used to his warmth, Adrian jerks his hand away, balling it into a fist and shoving it in his pocket.

"Adrian."

"We can't." He ends it and rubs a hand over his chin. "Are you ready to try again?"

I nod and take his arm. He doesn't offer, I just take it. I need support, to be taken away. Adrian doesn't protest as he leads me to the car once more. He lets me dictate the pace, slow even steps.

When we face the car again, I taste the bile rise in my throat.

"It's okay, Tove," he whispers. "I've got you."

"Promise?" I wheeze through frayed breaths.

"Promise." His grip tightens against me, his jaw set, his forest burning.

I push down the fear and gulp a lungful of air, my heart threatening to burst from my chest. "Let's go."

Adrian opens the door for me and I slip inside. The smell of disinfectant I thought I had left in the hospital follows me into the car as if it has been saturated into the seats and every surface.

Adrian rounds the car, his eyes locked on mine, never leaving me. Just as he promised. He slips in beside me and slots the keys into the ignition.

"Are you ready?"

I nod, unable to speak.

When the car comes to life I jerk and my hand grabs his thigh, my fingernails digging in, like a petrified cat inside a burning house.

"Just breathe Tove, I've got you."

His warm hand lands on mine and he doesn't pry my hand away. Instead, he wraps his fingers around mine and squeezes. We sit inside the car the engine humming around us.

"I've got you." His voice cracks and I look to his agonised face.

"I'm okay." I nod.

Adrian puts the car into gear, and we roll out of the parking space. My heart jolts and my stomach ties itself in knots. My rib cage is a vice, squeezing my lungs, my breaths are panicked and shallow.

And then there's the raw timber of his voice that cuts

through it all and soothes me like balm. "Breathe, Tove. I've got you." His hand closes around mine and warmth rushes through my body.

I find air.

Adrian drives slowly, taking slow-rolling turns and keeping five miles below the speed limit on straights. The world rolls by me. We pass cityscapes, ugly buildings scarring the skyline, a blurring of cars and black tar. Life has moved on without me, but I haven't moved at all. I have been living in my head for the past six weeks, grabbing on to slivers of fog and clinging on to Adrian. Just like now.

Adrian slows in front of a red brick building. It looms over us, casting a long shadow over the road. He yanks his hand away from mine and clutches the steering wheel, his knuckles blanching, his eyes locked on the man running towards the car.

"Just remember to breathe, Tove."

As soon as Adrian comes to a full stop, Tray pulls on the handle and hauls it open.

"Tove, you're home." He beams down at me.

My heart is in my throat as Tray stands at the car door. He waits, his toes tapping on the pavement. Like he has somewhere else to be.

I inhale deeply and turn to Adrian. "Are you coming?"

Adrian's fingers tighten around the steering wheel, his knuckles so white it's as if he's dipped them in bleach.

"I'm not sure that's a good idea." He keeps facing forwards.

"You promised."

His head swivels to me and I feel I've just hit him with a low blow. I don't care. I need him. He scrubs a hand over his pinched face and reaches for the door.

Tray holds out his hand. It hovers in front of me in invitation. I take it and he helps me out of the car then leads me towards the building, ignoring Adrian completely.

We push through a small ugly hallway. Fading post-boxes with black numbers decorate one wall while the elevator waits for us on the other.

Tray ushers me inside and Adrian follows. The elevator smells like day-old fish and the air is thick with tension. It weighs heavily on my chest as my shoulders rub against the two men. Two men who are nothing alike, one my past and the other? Running from a future, with me. Pushing me away. My fingers flicker to my scar and I pull my beanie lower over my forehead.

Tray pushes the front door and it creaks open.

"Welcome home Tove." He crosses the threshold and gestures to the living room.

I take a steeling breath and step inside, my eyes flickering around as if I'm trapped inside a pinball machine of furniture, lights, stuff.

"Are you remembering anything?" Tray sounds eager.

"Give her time." Adrian's voice drifts past me.

"No one fucking asked you, freak," Tray spits out.

I take another step inside. My eyes drift over the circular dining room table. It's empty. My finger slides against the wood, slick and smooth. Just beyond it is a couch. I examine it. Two cushions, bland and faded, only coloured by the sunshine drifting in from two back windows. The kitchen on the right is cramped and tidy, almost unused. Everything is devoid of colour and life– it's as though only ghosts live here.

"Where is all my stuff?"

"Everywhere."

I look around and shake my head.

"*My* stuff."

"This way." Tray gestures down a narrow corridor. "Our bedroom. The door on the left."

I take tentative steps towards the room, feeling two sets of eyes on my back, my heart thudding in my chest.

The bed is made with more creams and blacks. I wonder

why we live in black and white. It smells of boy. Old, stale drool and sweat and stinky socks. Tray.

In the corner, I notice cases and bags. I reach over.

"Your photography equipment. I wasn't sure what to do with it…" His voice falls away. I finger the cases and unzip a bag, inside I find a DSLR camera and zoom. I reach for the camera and hold it to my face. It feels heavy in my hand but also right, a piece that somehow fits perfectly in all the chaos.

I aim the camera at Tray. He smiles at me, pulling a face, his lips pout and his chin lifts. I click, he smiles, I click again.

I point the camera to Adrian. He doesn't smile. His eyes burn through the lenses, pensive and pained. I click. Something tugs inside me. I try to grasp the memory but it won't hold still.

I frown and search. "Do you remember something, Tove?" Tray is almost careful.

I shake my head, put the camera down on the bed and walk to my cupboard.

I open drawers of clothes. They don't interest me. I slide onto the floor and reach for the bottom drawer, the last unexplored space in this colourless existence.

The last drawer holds a large portfolio. I flick it open. Faces. Beautiful, ugly, sad, happy faces all look at me through pictures. Coloured and black and white photographs jump out at me from the pages, creases and scars, tears and laughter. Humanity is there in front of me, in all its damaged perfect self. And I know deep inside me that I have captured all those moments. I turn the pages, one after the other. They whisper to me, holding a secret so deep I need to find it.

I flick to the last page. And my heart seizes.

A black and white picture with a beautiful broken boy who stares back at me. He sits shirtless, leaning against a white wall, a hand resting on a bent knee, his eyes burning into the camera with the same pensive broken stare. A dried rose slide onto my lap, the once red petals almost black, the once full bloom shed to a few final blades.

My heart squeezes in my chest as I fight a lump that crawls up my throat, and my eyes shoot to Adrian. Our eyes lock.

"Adrian...?"

"Tove..." his face is full of ragged emotion, torn and frayed like my heart.

"Don't!" I swallow the emotion that threatens to rip me apart. "Who are you? To me?"

"Tove..."

"No! the truth! Why do I have this picture of you?" My heart seizes in my chest.

Tray scoffs, "You and Adrian go way back, even further back than you and me. He knows who you are, he's known who you are since you were kids—used to be your next-door neighbour. He's been obsessed with you for years."

Adrian's eyes fall away he looks weary and tired, the forest in his eyes dark.

"Adrian?" I search his face, looking for his eyes, but he won't look at me. "I don't understand what's going on."

Tray smirks. "What's going on is that he tracked you down, found you here, and he's trying to insert himself back into your life."

"Adrian?" My head swims in a fog of confusion, but I can feel all the words screaming at me, wanting to break through the wall.

"Answer me, damnit! Who are you to me? I need to know the truth!" I inhale the toxic air in the room and my body clinches with anger.

Adrian remains stoic, silent. He scratches his chin. He exchanges a look with Tray. I can see the darkness that flows between them and I wonder how much Tray hasn't told me.

His eyes finally land on mine. "Tove, I'm not in the mood." He sighs, as though he knows something.

"So what else is new?" The words spill from my mouth as if they knew the response.

Our eyes lock and I bolt up from the bed, my breath ragging in my throat, scratching it with force. The fog inside my head clears, and the wall collapses. The pieces of the puzzle slam into each other violently, pushing into place, creating the perfect picture—all the pictures. My head screams with pain as memories keep pushing inside it. A violent forceful deluge floods my mind. My hands clasp my chest, but the screams don't come. I dry heave, my chest compressing, my lungs collapsing, my heart shattering.

"Breathe, Tove." His smooth timber voice cuts through. "Just breathe."

I suck in long inhales, gasping at my new reality. I look up and see Adrian and for the first time I *see* Adrian, not just the man that sits beside me and strokes my back, but all the everythings that he's always been to me and meant to me. The boy, the scrawny bendy boy has turned into a man, strong and beautiful and incredible and a fucking liar, and all I want is to strangle him, and hate him, and kiss him, and have him. I suck in another broken breath and my eyes swing to Tray. The treacherous fuck. When our eyes meet, he flinches. He knows I know. They both know.

"You took this picture when we were seventeen." Adrian's voice slices me in half. "Your dad gave you the camera for your birthday. It was the first picture you ever took, even though I told you that you should only take pictures of beautiful things." He swallows away the memory.

"I want you to leave," I whisper.

"Tove, I don't think that's such a good ide—"

Adrian doesn't finish. Tray grabs him and flings him into the wall. "Get away from her you freak! She told you to leave."

Tray swings a fist wildly and it connects with Adrian's face with brutal force.

Adrian's grimaces, his face tears and pulls and he snarls, pushing Tray away. He grips him by the collar of his shirt and spins him pinning him the wall, his fist curling.

"Stop." I growl, it's carnal and savage and broken. Adrian's face snaps back to me, his forest stark and haunted.

Grief engulfs me, like a snake. It slithers around me choking me and I feel as though I am being torn apart, dying. There is so much pain. So much anger that seethes through me. The betrayal stings and cuts so deeply. I can almost forgive Tray, because he was always a liar, it was in his nature. Somehow Adrian's omission is worse than lying.

"You should've said something." My voice quivers and my body shakes, as sharp pain pierces my brain. Adrian's fist smashes the wall inches from Trays head. He grunts heavily and releases Tray.

Adrian wipes his top lip with his sleeve and it comes back with a bloody stain. The rivulet of blood streaks down his chin, spilling into his scar, colouring it like a bloody river.

Adrian's broken face looks at mine while Tray's face is marred in an angry scowl. He looks like a beast, an ugly demented thing.

"I want you *both* to leave," I manage through the anger, the pain.

"No Tove, no listen…" Tray starts but Adrian grips him by the collar and drags him to the door, "I can explain, just let me expla-" he doesn't finish as Adrian shoves him outside.

I can hear raised voices, angry shouts and then a door slams.

Adrian's face reappears at the door. "I'll call Doctor Jäger." Our eyes lock and his are full of sorrow. His face is drawn, he opens his mouth as if to speak. I look away. I don't care. Except that I do. When I look up again, he's gone.

The tears start falling, as if the flood inside my head has broken through a dam and the deluge is forcing its way out through my tear ducts, pushing everything out. Raw, unadulterated pain and sorrow. I am a broken vessel.

I'm tired and in pain, all the wrong sorts of pain and I'm all alone, I'm so fucking alone. The sobs rip through my chest, and the memories are sinking into my head, ingraining themselves deeply inside me once again. I remember *everything*.

Tove

"How are you feeling today?" Doctor Jäger stands by my side as we stare into the garden.

"Better, thank you."

"Good, good." I catch a flicker of a smile in his reflection.

"Everything kind of trickled back after the other day." I stop and swallow a lump in my throat. "It still hasn't really stopped. I still have blanks, I can feel them, but the big picture is there."

"That's wonderful, Tove. And I have more wonderful news. I am going to let you go home."

I turn to the doctor and he beams at me. "Really?"

"With your back healed and your memory back there's no reason for you to remain here. We have arranged for a nurse to escort you and a new physiotherapist to do home visits."

I nod and curl my hands around me.

"Now remember, we still don't know if there is long term permanent damage, so you will come and see me once a week, for the foreseeable future." He beams at me as if we are good friends arranging coffee dates. "You must look after yourself, because the side effects of your trauma will likely follow you for a number of months if not years."

"Side effects?"

"You know, your balance and mood swings, the occasional lost conversation." He pats me on the shoulder. "It will be okay though."

I want to agree, but all I feel is petrified and totally alone.

Since I woke up at the hospital there has been no sign of Tray or Adrian. I feel myself scanning the garden, looking for a familiar face. I scoff at myself. Even the ones I thought were familiar turned out to be total strangers.

I tune back in to Doctor Jäger. "...I'll have the nurses finish off the paperwork and you'll be free to go. Look after yourself, Miss Savage."

"Thank you, Doctor Jäger."

He leaves unceremoniously and I feel my knees shake. I collapse on the bed and allow myself one last cry.

⁓

The apartment feels untouched. I don't know if Tray returned after the ambulance staff hauled me out of there. I walk through the rooms and wish I could forget all over again.

Forget Tray in the bed with some chick, licking her pussy. Forget every excuse I ever told myself to stay with him. Forget the wasted years I spent with that prick. Forget all his lies that permeate my skin. I want to shower, I want to get clean of him. I don't know if I can ever wash him away, his touch, his smell, his kisses. Bile rises in my throat and I push it down, batting away the thoughts. I promised myself I wouldn't dwell.

I shower, dress, and try to rediscover my apartment. There's too much Tray here. Too much history. I need a fresh start, but first, I need to recuperate. I need to rest my broken mind and let my body heal, and allow myself to forget all the things I actually want to forget and remember the things that were good and special and wonderful. Like the way Adrian's fingers fluttered over my belly, or the way his fingers gripped my skin, and the way his body felt against mine and the way his timber voice pierced right into my core and made everything feel warm and safe.

I swat my thoughts away and consider my options. I pick up the phone. An hour later, I have a plan.

I'm going home. Dad could never bear to sell it and has been asking me for years to move back in. A housekeeper comes in once a week to maintain the property. He's ecstatic when I ask.

I pull up the first box and start packing. I spend the day emptying cupboards, leaving Tray's shit on the floor, He can pack up on his own.

I grab my phone and call Tray, who picks up after the first ring.

"Tove—"

"Shut up and listen," I cut him off, hearing his sharp inhale. "I'm leaving the apartment tonight. I've cancelled the lease. I suggest you come and get your shit tomorrow, because the realtor will collect the keys on Friday."

"Tove, don't do this—"

I hang up. My phone starts the flash, Tray's name screaming from the screen. I ignore it. I've said everything I'm ever going to say to King Douche. I chuckle, then frown as my body clenches. I need to stop thinking about those things.

My body aches with exhaustion, my back hurts and muscles burn. A train of boxes litters the floor. They will be collected in the morning.

I lower myself to the floor and catch a glimpse of an object under the bed. I reach for it. It is my portfolio, lying discarded like a dead bird, its wings spread open. I flip through the pages. Faces look back at me. Each tells a story, beautiful moments captured with one click.

My insides constrict as I reach the last picture. Adrian's eyes burn into mine, his face twisted with tortured emotion. I flip to the final page and find a handwritten note.

'So what else is new.'

I clutch the portfolio to my chest as the sobs come again.

Adrian

HR were more than generous when they suggested paid leave. Two weeks away from the hospital, away from Tray and Tove and heartache. It was what I needed. Space, distance, alcohol. I didn't know what was worse, the fact that she remembered me or that look in her eyes, that one that screamed betrayal. I shouldn't care, not really, not given everything she put me through. Yet our hearts feel anchored together, both sinking to the bottom together, searching for air, screaming into the void.

My phone screeches through my thoughts, bringing them to a violent stop. I look at the screen and suck in a long breath.

"Hello."

"Hi Adrian." She stumbles over her awkwardness. "It's Kate."

"I know."

She huffs into the phone.

"Did you need something? Is Dad okay?"

"Oh, yes, he is, sorry to worry you. It's just that, erm…" I can imagine her trying to grasp words from thin air. "Your dad asked me to marry him last night." I can feel her holding her breath, seeking my approval, as if I hold her happiness in a closed case above my bed and only I can set it free.

"What did you say?"

"Yes, of course." She breathes out the words and I can taste her happiness. It spews through the phone and into my ear and makes my body churn with jealous anger.

"Congratulations," I grate. It's not my fault I'm poisoned again. I have bitten Tove's apple and my veins are pumping the toxins through my body. Jealousy, anger, guilt - a noxious concoction that makes me the beast she's always wanted me to be. I clear my throat, because Kate deserves better. "I mean it, I hope you guys will be happy together." And I do mean it.

She sighs into the phone. The silence drifts back and forth between our breaths.

"Was there anything else?"

"Yes, actually." I can hear her hesitation. "We would like you to come for the weekend, to celebrate with us."

"I'm not…"

"Please." She cuts me off before I can find an excuse.

I slam my eyes shut. "Okay."

"Great, thank you, we'll see you tomorrow."

She hangs up before I can say anything more and I moan into the room. I grab my backpack and stuff some clothes into it. Maybe after the visit home I can take a road trip. Go back to the mountains, hike and breathe and just be. I chuck my backpack by the door and go for a jog, hoping the fresh air will clear my head, but all it does is make me spend more time with my thoughts. The scalding shower washes away my sweat and eases my burning muscles but does nothing for the quake inside me, the unrelenting wave of regret.

I don't eat. I sleep like shit.

It's going to be a long weekend.

"Sorry I'm late."

Dad opens the door and his face breaks into a smile. I should have been here hours ago, but my detour took longer than expected.

"Don't be silly, I'm glad you're here."

He doesn't scold me, he never has, even when I deserved it. He leads me to the dining room where an unimpressed Kate sits with her arms crossed.

"Look who's here," Dad says and pats me on the back as he grabs my backpack and throws it on the couch.

"Well it's about bloody time." Kate shows no restraint. "I knew you'd be late, but for fuck sakes, Adrian, it's almost nine, dinner is cold and crusty, and you're being rude. If you were going to be this late you should have called.'

"Kate!" My dad wants to defend me, to let me get away with it as he always has.

"No, she's right, it was a dick move. Sorry." I scrub a hand over my face. "Things just got away from me…"

"Things?"

"Time." I correct myself, but Kate's eyes narrow.

"Is everything okay?" She scrutinises my face while my dad's gaze flickers from my face to hers as though he's watching a tennis match between two old rivals that share a drink after a match.

"It will be. I need to get away. I'll stay till Sunday and then take off for a while to clear my head… if that's okay with you — me staying that is." I feel sheepish asking but she's made herself the woman of this household.

"Of course, Adrian, stay as long as you need." Her anger dissipates, replaced by worry.

Dinner is cold and crusty just as Kate said it would be, but it's also easy and warm in a way it's never been before. They're not pretending anymore, all the eggshells have been swept away and we fall out of the dark corner and into a comfortable beat where normalcy lives, as if it's always been this easy.

I thank Kate for dinner and apologise again for fucking it up and offer to do the washing up as my penance. She shoos me away with a kitchen towel and a smile. I dodge Dad by telling him I'm just too tired to talk, and climb the stairs to my room.

I lie in the darkness, the bed cradling my aching body, sleep beckoning me, a welcome siren song, and then a square of light flickers to life on my wall. I bolt from the bed and look through my window. The lights in Tove's room are on.

I creep in the darkness and watch the empty space, waiting, and then there she is, Tove, in her fucking room.

Fuck.

I roll away from my window and consider my options. *Fuck.*

I grab my phone and reach for the light switch.

I flick the light on, giving her the signal, then wait three long agonising breaths before my fingers type out the message.

'Come to the window.'

I stand in the middle of the frame, waiting. My body tenses and hardens with each passing second, uncertainty filtering inside me like weak coffee. And then there she is, her beautiful face furrowed and angry.

She reaches for her phone. **'What are u doing here?'**

I read the message and watch my phone's battery, the 1% mocking me. I start to type and the screen dies.

Fuck.

I hold my phone up and cross a finger under my neck. She nods her understanding. I hold both palms up and pray she won't go anywhere while I dig around my old desk. I find a pile of papers and markers in the bottom drawer, pull them out and scribble in my best bad writing. **'Kate and Dad got engaged.'**

She stares at the paper and looks up at my face. All I can see is the anger as she shoots daggers at me from across the courtyard.

We stare at each other through the panes, the distance between us an uncrossable chasm. When she remains motionless, I grab another paper. **'I'm sorry.'**

It's not good enough, but I plaster the paper against the window, she looks at the words, stands up and walks away. I let the paper drop to the floor like a dead autumn leaf and lean against the cold pane.

Fuck.

I stare at the empty space and my heart aches, my breath fogging the glass. My body constricts with longing with remorse.

Movement catches my eye. Tove is back. She sits down, holding some paper and a marker.

She pulls the lid off and sucks at her lower lip, concentrating as she writes.

My body shudders with anticipation, with long-lost memories.

'You lied.' She smashes the paper against the pane, her eyes fierce and angry.

I scrub a hand over my face. What am I meant to say? I didn't lie, I just didn't tell her.

She pulls the page away even as my mind churns with a response and she flips the page over. **'You should have told me.'**

'I tried.'

'Not hard enough.'

My face pinches. She doesn't give me a chance to answer.

'You hurt me.'

She seems so fragile, like a broken porcelain doll glued together unevenly. I suck in a deep breath and grab the paper, scribbling.

It was the time for the truth. **'I wanted to.'**

'To punish me?'

'Yes.'

I hang my head as I watch a tear roll down her cheek.

'**Are we even now?**'

'**No.**'

I growl and shake my head and all I want is to reach out to her. Touch her, comfort her.

'**No.**' I push the paper against the pane again more violently. I search my pile. '**I'm sorry.**'

She just stares at me, her face a mask of agony.

'**I was wrong.**'

I scribble like a madman. '**I thought I wanted to hurt you.**'

'**You did.**' She holds out the words and the writing isn't neat and round, it's jagged and angry and stained with tears.

'**But it's not what I want now.**'

'**So, what do you want, Adrian?**'

'**You. I've only ever wanted you.**'

I hold the paper to the window and she reads over the lines. I can see her eyes scan them over and over and my heart wants to smash through the window and fly into her body, to make her feel all the things it feels, to flow through her.

Instead, she shakes her head. '**It's too late.**'

She writes and holds the paper to the window and my heart falls into the endless void of my stomach. It drops and keeps dropping because it feels as though there is no bottom. This new empty pain, this ache, will never go away.

I scramble through my pile of papers and grab it. '**No!**'

I bang the glass and push the paper against it. "No!" I shout and shake my head at her. Her eyes drop away and her paper falls to the floor like discarded snow and she stands up. Our eyes lock for a second, an endless desperate second, and then she's gone.

The lights go out in her room and I am staring into the darkness.

In the morning, Dad wants to spend time and be a family, he wants to talk about the wedding, he asks me to be his best man. I try to concentrate on his words but my mind drifts to Tove's room, to her bedroom, to her last words to me. I need to see her, tell her, touch her, show her just how I feel.

I stay with Dad because I'm trying to glue together all my relationships. Everything in my life feels cracked, like dry clay that's been left in the sun too long. I'm trying to heal, to mend. So I stay and I listen and I try to smile and I force enthusiasm and I sit through lunch, till Kate says she needs something from town and I talk Dad into driving her.

When they're gone, I round the fence and stand at Tove's door. The house hasn't changed. Dad says there are care-takers that come and look after the place. Maybe Richard still held out hope to one day bring his wife back here. To live. To die.

I knock on the door. It goes unanswered. I try again. Silence.

I pound and call her name, but still there's only the birds and the breeze that answer me. I try the knob and the door falls open. I push it wider and light falls over the foyer.

"Tove?" I call as I step inside. The house is furnished but it feels abandoned, it's too crisp and clean. It doesn't have that lived in feeling of warmth, but the sterile stale air of some-thing just barely alive. I step further into the house.

"Tove?"

I call again and strain my ears. Silence.

I take the stairs two at a time, my stomach lurches with the memory of the last time I ran up these stairs. The door to her room is closed. I knock again. When there's no answer I open it and find the room much like the rest of the house, abandoned.

I step inside. The air here is different, more alive and I can smell her. Like a rose, delicate and sweet, she's everywhere as if her smell permeates the walls. My eyes sweep over the room, it's barren and feels too small. My eyes land on the window. I look through and stare at my room, an empty shell waiting for an occupant that never wanted to be there.

I turn to walk away and then I see it. A pile of smashed dry leaves. Deep red, broken and scattered over a single piece of paper. My heart sinks. I read the words again,

'It's too late.'

I step out of her room and out of her house and convince myself that I will forget Tove Savage.

Adrian

I shake the cobwebs in my head and splash water on my face. Another packed day at the hospital. My days have been filled with broken people. I try and keep my focus on them. To keep my mind inside a box of pain. Other people's pain, so I don't get swept away by my own.

Losing Tove for a second time was more devastating than the first. It felt deeper somehow, more brutal, more raw. Maybe because it was different this time, because she wanted it as much as I did. I swipe the memories away like chalk on a board.

Winter is almost finished, and the world is almost warmer again. The sun paints it in her golden colours and brings with it warmth and new beginnings. I wish I could enjoy it more.

I park my car and walk through the hospital garden. It smells like roses, the smell suffocating me, curdling in my stomach. I don't watch where I am going when I walk into the man.

"Watch where you're going." His voice clips and I recognise it straight away. Our eyes lock, *"freak."*

His hand is wrapped around a woman's shoulder and her belly protrudes, rounded and beautiful. Her caramel skin glows and her hands caress the bump with elongated fingers.

"What are you looking at, freak? Coming to steal another woman from me?"

I scoff, "I never stole anyone from you, Tray. Look at us! No one would ever pick me over you."

"*She* did."

"No. She didn't."

He looks at me and for the first time I see pity there. I preferred the hatred. "If you believe that, you're even more stupid than you look. She was never mine, she was never anyone's but yours."

I stand there and as I look at him, my heart cramps in my chest. "Well, it's over now, she's gone."

"She's here."

I swallow the words.

"On twenty-fifth and fourth, she has a studio there."

Tray looks at me and his mouth pulls in a half smile, making him look like something resembling a human being. "Good luck, freak." He doesn't say anything more, just leads the woman away.

She's asking him questions as they walk towards the hospital doors and he shakes his head.

The day drags like chains on a prisoner. Except that I am the prisoner and the weight of my chains threatens to suffocate me.

When my last session ends, I run to my car through air that feels thick and humid. Cloud are gathering or maybe that's just the thoughts in my head, clouded, unsure.

One last chance to make her mine and keep her.

I drive to a craft shop around the corner and grab some

cardboard and markers. I spend the next half hour preparing. I have to do this right, this one time.

One last time.

The air feels charged as if the sky is about to rip apart.

I park outside the building, a two-story shop front with an apartment above. I bet she's happy here. I sit in my car and watch, looking for any signs of her, but it's past closing time, and the sky has darkened.

I pull out my phone and my cards and take a galvanising breath. I start texting.

'Come to the window.'

I hold my breath as I wait. Her face bursts beyond the curtain of the upstairs room and her eyes are wide, her face painted with shock.

'How did you find me?' she texts, but I ignore her, tucking the phone into my pants. I'm going to say what I have to say, and she is going to read it.

I grab the cardboards and hold the first one up.

'I'm sorry I fucked up.'

She folds her hands across her body.

'I'm a coward.'

'It's not too late.'

I flip through my boards, one at a time, her face set as she reads,

'I was angry all the time, at you.'

'I lied because I wanted to punish you.'

'It's no excuse.'

'You broke my heart and it stayed broken.'

'But when I saw you again, it stirred something in me.'

'I know you feel it too.'

'I love you Tove. I think you love me too.'

'You make me feel unbroken.'

'Forgive me.'

I'm a ball of nervous energy, the storm inside me like the

one brewing above. She looks at me with those icy eyes and I don't know if it's glaciers or fire.

The first fat drop of rain smashes against my shoulder and stains my shirt, another follows into my hair, another and another. I am pelted by the freezing rain, as thunder crackles above me, but I keep standing, the sign slowly disintegrating in my arms, crumbling under the weight of the water. Still we stand, two unmovable statues. Her arms fall to her side and then she is gone.

I blow out a heavy sigh and my heart splinters. I let the ruined sign fall at my feet and turn to my car when I hear the creak of the door. She stands there, leaning against the frame, her blazing blue eyes hiding an agitated tempest, drowning me, taunting me.

She stands aside, letting the door fall open in a silent invitation. I hesitate as I cross the street, a few more uncertain steps then stagger over the threshold.

❧

Tove

Adrian is drenched, his hair stuck to his forehead in clumps, his clothes glued to his body like a second skin. Water glistens off his day-old stubble, he looks tired, he looks beautiful. We're at a standoff, an impasse, deadlocked.

"What took you so long?"

He stands there, brooding, pensive, then swipes the wet clumps of hair from his face.

I can feel his need. It collides with my own as waves of desire spill from us both and crash inside the room. I can't breathe, my chest tightens around my lungs. I am dragged under his flood waters and then we rush.

My pulse surges and my heart churns and then his lips slam against mine and his desperate groans fill my lungs. His arms cage me against him, and his wet clothes soak through mine, and I don't care because I can't stop kissing him, touching him, drowning in him.

His fingers slip under the hem of my shirt and creep along my back, leaving searing trails in their wake. His nails dig and bite into my skin, ripping me apart.

He pulls away from me and I wrench my eyes open. The forest of his eyes is hooded, darkness awaits beneath the canopy.

His thumb sweeps over my lips and I suck at it just to taste if he's left a bit of himself behind. I grab his shirt and peel it from his body, it falls with a splatter to the floor. I slide my hands down his broad shoulders, carving out a path down to his belt. I rip it open and claw at his zipper, tugging the saturated pants away from him. I fall to my knees and pull the jeans away, they land in a heap by the wasted shirt. I look up at Adrian. His eyes burn with hunger. My fingers creep along his legs and slip inside the waistband of his underwear. He rasps but makes no move to stop me.

I pull away at his boxers and stare at the pulsing rigid cock. I flick my tongue against the head, and he growls low in his chest. The sounds sets me alight as if I've just been struck by lightning. I suck him into my mouth.

"Fuck, Tove." He sounds raw, broken, desperate.

His fingers sink into my hair as I indulge in his desire. His rasping breaths are low and sharp and his hips grind against my mouth, his fists tighten in my hair, twisting and pulling, his back falls against the wall and his head tilts to the ceiling.

"Stop," he grates, but I don't, I want him, to have him, control him, taste him. He yanks my hair and he falls from my mouth with an agonised groan. He sinks to his knees and I back away. He stalks forwards, his body glistening with sweat and rain and I want to lick him dry.

I scramble back and still he stalks forward, crawling

behind me like a hungry desperate wolf, and I know that is what he is, starving.

His hand closes around my foot and he yanks, halting my retreat, "Tove." His timber voice is edged with desperate need. "Don't run from me again."

I nod, frozen beneath him. He bats away the hair from my face and his eyes follow the long line of my scar, his lips graze the ugly mark, and my heart stalls.

His lips find mine and the kiss is almost hesitant, slow and burning, and my body catches fire, his making me burn through my clothes.

His hand glides beneath my shirt, his fingers rip at my skin, he tears the shirt from me, and his mouth traces the curve of my jaw, the long arc of my neck, the harsh line of my collar bone. He slips off the straps of my bra, and tugs until my breasts fall from the cups. Adrian groans, a wretched strained sound that makes my body quiver with a desperate ache.

His tongue flicks at my nipple, nothing more than a whisper of a sensation and yet I feel it everywhere. We moan together as he takes it into his mouth, his tongue swirling and nipping, relentless. I gulp for air as his teeth punish me.

Adrian grazes my skin once more, trailing kisses along my torso, the grotesque broken cavity of scarred tissue. I am paralysed as he kisses every inch of it, his eyes locked on mine. I suck in breath at the touch, somehow more intimate than I thought it would be, somehow intrusive yet comforting.

He slides my underwear aside and his stubble scrapes my thighs as his tongue lashes with feathery caresses, slow agonising strokes that skim and dip and swirl. My breathing falters and my hips grind against his face, seeking out every bit of electric friction. Heat spreads inside me and my hands are in his hair, thick and lush. I want to draw him nearer, harder, but he resists, his tongue sinfully playful at its own pace, tormenting, scorching.

"Adrian…" His name escapes in a broken rasp and he moves away from me. I whimper at the disconnection, instantly missing his heat.

His mouth finds mine, and heat floods my body as he kisses me, so gently, beautifully, breathing me in.

He rolls above me, his eyes exploring my face, the forest in his promises wilderness behind the gentle touches.

I gasp as he slips himself into me, and he growls in that broken way of his, that speaks to my soul, like only it can mend it.

I close my eyes, feeling him, drowning in him, memorising every sensation as his body smoulders against me. He bites my lip as his hips grind against mine.

"Look at me Tove," his voice rasps above me as he moves, slowly, in cruel gentle strokes that send waves of pleasure everywhere. Every nerve in my body screams for more, for less, for release. I am a tight rubber band being pulled apart, and my body craves more of it, more of him.

Thunder claps and lightning sets the dark room alight. Adrian transforms with the storm, he brings the tempest to my body, an unrelenting deluge. He moves inside me, dangerous, violent, hungry and I moan, my body ready to breach its dams, ready to spill across everything and swallow the world in my path.

Grunting, he sinks his hands into my hips and smashes into me as I break, and wave after wave of blazing pleasure washes through me, flooding my insides, and I scream and he howls and we crack and we mend and we are the same tangled beast, drenched in sweat and desire and forgiveness.

My senses are as frayed as my nerves. My body sticks to the cold wooden floor, wanting to melt into it. I am a puddle of sweat and pleasure and bewilderment.

The storm around us calms, the flood, a trickle of emotion that puddles around us.

Adrian braces on the floor and his eyes bore into me, his face torn in delight and despair.

He kisses me again. A soft tender kiss. "Are you okay?"

I nod. My lungs slowly remember how to hold air and push it out again, my skin tingles with his feathery touch.

I feel his warm breath on my shoulders and my lips ache for his.

"How did you find me?" I don't recognise my own voice.

"Tray."

"Tray?"

"I ran into him and his…" He swipes a hand around his jaw, sweeping the fine stubble. "He told me where to find you."

I know we share the same thought and Adrian sits up offering me his hand. I watch the muscles of his forearm flex as he pulls me up.

"I've hurt you so much haven't I?" I pull my knees to my chest, painfully aware of my mangled body.

He scrubs a hand over his face and pulls his full bottom lip into his mouth, "Tove?" He looks at me with those piercing sad eyes and his forest looks dark again, closing in on itself. "Is *this* what you want? Me? …Us?"

My lips quiver. "It's what I always wanted, Adrian, I've just been too stupid, too arrogant." A sob climbs up my throat. "I've just let other people's opinions dictate my choices."

"Tove…"

"No! Let me finish." I wipe the tears from my cheeks as they fall unhindered. "I've said and done terrible things to you, when all I should have said is that I love you, only you. Always you."

His fingers trace the curve of my jaw and his forest is burning. "It's always been you, Tove."

His lips crash into mine and the fire of his forest scorches my face, my skin, my everything and Adrian Rose sets me alight.

⚓

Adrian

The morning light filtering through the window wakes me. It dances across the wall and over Tove's sleeping face. I resist the urge to touch her, rather enjoying watching her, the slight twitch of her mouth as she breathes, the way the hair falls around her and the pink scar that tracks along her scalp.

I look around the small room. A walk-in closet, a tallboy, a bed side table with a lamp and a single framed picture. I pick it up and run my hand over the glass. A black and white portrait of a boy with a broken face looks back at me, like going back in time and looking at a mirror for the very first time.

"You're just as beautiful now," her voice croaks, and is full of sleep.

"I was never beautiful."

"You've always been the most beautiful person I ever knew."

"I used to think that about you, too."

"Used to?" Her hands jerks to her scar.

I sink my fingers into her hair and my lips find hers, full of invitation. I kiss her, hard, my tongue sweeps past her lips and she moans into my mouth, unravelling pieces of me.

"You'll always be beautiful Tove, but you made me realise that life is only beautiful because it's full of ugly moments. You took my ugly moments and turned them into something amazing, time after time. You'll always be so much more than beautiful, Tove."

She draws me to her and our lips mash together, and the morning is spent creating an artwork of our design. Twisted bodies and mangled limbs, grinding, licking, clawing. We make music, a gasping, moaning duet. We are creators of beautiful destructive things, violent, gentle things, cruel pleasurable masterpieces, until we lie wasted and broken, glued together with sweat and heat and love.

Adrian

I straighten his tie for the third time, and he grasps at it again as if it's choking him.

"You don't have to wear it, Dad," I say, and he looks at me as if I'm mad.

"It looks good. You look good."

"Yeah?"

"Hey, Dad, relax, she already said yes, she's been planning this day for six months, or maybe longer. Stop being so nervous. It will be okay."

He stills and his eyes find mine, then he drags a hand over his clean-shaven chin. "Will it?"

I sigh. "Mum's been dead for almost twenty years." It's true, but he still flinches at my words as if I whipped him. "You're not cheating on her, and you're not betraying her. She probably wanted you to have this sooner."

He closes the distance between us and kisses my cheek, then draws me in. "She would have been so proud of the man you've become."

He breaks the hug and I wipe my eyes. "We'd better get going."

He squeezes my shoulder once more as if I'm the one needing the reassurance, and we step outside, where the dying sunlight sears my eyes. In the last week I've worked nonstop, ensuring Kate and Dad get the wedding of their dreams. Our backyard has been transformed into a mini wonderland. White chairs adorn the freshly cut lawn and a white canopy flaps lazily in the breeze, fairy lights twinkling along the poles and across the fabric as the sun dips beyond the horizon.

In the darkness, the garden comes to life, lights twinkle and illuminate the night.

I stand behind my father, who bounces on his heels, his fingers entwined, locked behind his back. Music begins playing and the guests stand up as Kate walks down the makeshift aisle. I'm sure she looks pretty in her white dress, but I only have eyes for Tove.

She looks stunning as she smiles at me, a bright red dress hugging her body and her jet-black hair, styled in a wave across her head, cascading to one side, the other shaved to show off her scar. She takes my breath away. She's always taken my breath away.

The ceremony is beautiful, full of laughter and joy and love. It is encapsulated in our garden, my boyhood home, in the faces of each of the guests, a great big gushy bubble of love. It's sickly and sweet and I'm happy for them.

The guests are ushered away into the marquee to enjoy some canapes while Dad and Kate go to have their pictures taken.

"Everything looks so beautiful," Tove gushes as she falls into my arms.

"Nothing here is nearly as beautiful as you."

Her hand flinches to her face and falls before she could trace her permanent accessory. She could have hidden it, but she doesn't. It makes me love her so much more. I kiss her lips, swept by a sudden desire to have her right then, to claim her as mine.

I yank her by the arm and pull her towards the house.

"Where are we going?"

"I'm hungry."

"There's food in the...."

"That's not what I'm craving right now," I growl at her.

She swallows and her cheeks flush. I lead her past the caterers milling around in the kitchen and haul her up the stairs to my room, possessed by a need that defies reason.

I slam the door shut, pinning Tove to it with my body, my mouth capturing hers in a possessive, savage, kiss. I fall to my knees.

"Adrian..." She tries to stop me as I pull up her long dress and crawl beneath the ruffles. My hands creep up her legs and my fingers sneak inside her underwear, stealing the air from her lungs.

I bury myself between her legs, her scent rising to torment me. My tongue inflicts its leisurely cruelty on her, her voice breaks and her body shivers. I dine on her like the beast that I am, insatiable, hungry, wild. I can't get enough of her smell, her taste, the feel of her skin, sticky against my face.

She whimpers my name and my skin ignites. I will deal with those needs later. Now I just need Tove. I want to make her face contort and grimace and twist. I don't need to see it. I know her face now, all the broken faces she makes as I give her pleasure. The ugly truth that lies behind her beauty, when she is stripped down and raw. She moans and whimpers, her body shivers around me, her thighs clamp together, her body sinking, her legs failing her. And still my tongue flicks and carves and swirls until she can bear no more, her hips grinding against my greedy mouth as her raspy voice utters my name like a prayer. I take from her all that she is willing to give and then release her.

She is breathless, flushed skin and red lips. All mine.

"I love you," I whisper to her.

"I love too, Adrian." She smiles down at me, her body resting along the wall.

I remain on my knees in the place I can worship her. I pull out the folded piece of paper I prepared earlier that day and open it up, holding it in front of her.

'Will you marry me, Tove?'

Her hands fly to her mouth and her fingertips graze her scar. "Of course I will."

I stand and place the ring on her finger and my mouth slams into hers. I know she can taste herself and the thought makes me harder.

"Adrian," she moans into my mouth and I nearly crumple.

"We need to re-join the party, before the bride and groom start wondering where we are."

She licks her lips and nods. "I can't wait to tell them."

"I can't wait to fuck you." I nibble her neck and she pushes me away.

"All in good time, you insatiable beast."

I growl at her and she giggles. "Is this beauty going to make this beast beg?"

"Probably." She smirks and I want to wipe it from her mouth and turn it into a twisted tortured expression of plea-sure. I lick my lips, savouring the image.

I pull the rose from my tuxedo and place it in her hair.

"I can't wait to make you mine."

"You never have to wait, Adrian, I have always been yours."

ACKNOWLEDGMENTS

A Word from Jane:

I would like to start by thanking you, the reader, so much for reading! If you enjoyed the story, please leave a review and recommend the book to any friend you think would love Tove and Adrian's story. You will have my eternal love and gratitude. Even a few short words go a long way.

As always, I would love to thank my wonderful friend and beta Dawn, her enthusiasm knows no boundaries, her genuine love for books, reading, and helping authors is contagious and humbling. I have loved having her in my corner. Thank you.

A massive thank you Jennifer Demeter who created my beautiful cover! You're amazing and I can't wait to work with you again.

To all my other betas and C/Ps, your input and critiques have been invaluable. Without you, I would not be where I am today.

ABOUT THE AUTHOR

Jane Wynters doesn't quite know how to answer the question of where are you from? She's moved from place to place like a snowflake on the wind always searching for a safe place to land. She loves meeting new people and exploring new places. She loves reading, writing and conjuring new worlds from her imagination. Coffee is at the top of her food pyramid and she is fluent in three languages, her favourite being sarcasm.

Want to know more about the author and keep in touch? Get snippets of upcoming books and have a bit of twisted fun?

Come join me in Wonderland